Mr Daynty's Maiden Voyage

By

John D. Ross-Williams

Edited

By

John Rossiter

Table of Contents

Forward

By
John Rosssiter

This book is part of a series of short stories written by my late Father who sadly died aged 86 after a few years suffering from Dementia.

I was well aware that he was a keen writer and he was a member of The Mold Writers Guild for many years prior to his illness and deterioration. After his death, I was responsible for clearing his belongings and came across an old laptop that he used to write his stories, so I took a look and found hundreds of stories he had written some only a few pages long and others, like this one, a bit longer. In addition he had also written a full novel called "Urchins By The Canal". At the time of writing this, I am in the process of editing and formatting it ready for publishing.

My Father was born in December 1933 in St Asaph, North Wales, but as a toddler he was sent to an orphanage near Liverpool. He joined the Merchant Navy at the age of 15 and worked initially as a cabin boy for the Blue Funnel Line owned by Alfred Holt Ltd. By the time he was 19, he had been around the world 3 times and when he left his last ship in Vancouver, Canada, travelled alone across Canada via the Canadian Pacific Railroad to Halifax Nova Scotia, where he joined another ship to take him back to Liverpool. Now I don't know any 19 year olds today that can say they have done that.

He was a great Father and an inspiration to me and I used to love hearing his tales of exotic ports. I have included all his notes in the appendix that are well worth reading after having read the book.

He always wanted to be published but never had the opportunity, so here we are Dad, you are finally a published writer.

CHAPTER 1

Mr Daynty Sets Sail

The carriage pulled up at the gangway of the clipper tied up along-side the Liverpool Alfred quay. The three tall masts were gently swaying from side to side but nobody seemed to notice the movement. A young clean faced, tousled haired Zackary Daynty alighted from the carriage that had left the Manse in Tarmley Edge, Cheshire, very early that morning. The carriage driver put the lad's kit bag down on the cobbled stones together with his tightly rolled-up paillasse. The paillasse had been filled with down feathers at his father's insistence as befitting the status of a young and budding officer rather than with straw used by the common sailor. Zac thanked the driver and the carriage turned around and headed back to Cheshire. Zak had never seen such hustle and bustle like this in his life before. Horses and carts came and went leaving their cargos in the charge of Mr Fallowfield who represented the owners of the clipper, 'Sea Breeze'. There was a hurdy-gurdy playing the same tune over and over again somewhere out of his line of sight that lent a certain incongruity to the entire scene....

The lower yardarms were being used as cranes to lift cargo aboard the ship from the quayside. The purchase rope threaded its way through a series of blocks and pulleys ending up around the windlass that was manned by several sailors. Zak had never smelt so many aromas in one place before and they posed a challenge to his senses. He tried to distinguish each of them in his mind but some were stronger than others. There was a strong smell of rum and Demerara sugar and mixed spices he couldn't put a name to. However, he couldn't mistake the tang of fine mature Cheshire and Double Gloucester cheese which was just discernable under the over riding back-ground stink of horse manure and tar. He figured the smell of the place must change from day to day depending on what the ship was loading or discharging at the time. It occurred to him that the port probably handled goods from every corner of the world all of which lent to the excitement of the place.

Zak Daynty was sixteen years old and hailed from the country. He was the youngest son of the Reverend Joshua Daynty, the vicar of St Mark's of Tarmley Edge in rural Cheshire. One of the vicar's wealthy parishioners held an interest in the Caribbean Shipping Line and had arranged with Captain Oakley, the master of the 'Sea Breeze', to take the lad under his wing. He would 'teach him the ropes' so to speak with a view to the lad eventually buying a commission in the navy. Zak Daynty had never seen a real ship before and as he cast his eyes along its length he guessed it must have measured at least 165 feet long. As he cast his eyes over this new and exciting scene he knew he was in for some kind of high adventure. He saw sailors scrubbing the decks, mending torn sails and deftly wielding their marlin spikes while splicing bollard eyes at the end of new ropes. It never occurred to him that a ship of this size required a crew of well over 160 men to man it. He noted two men on boson's chairs hanging over the forward end while calking between the curving bow-planks with strips of oakum. Others were guiding swinging nets of cargo aboard and lowering it down the hatch where others stowed it in its designated place.

Someone shouted from the cross-tree of the main mast and Zak's gaze was drawn aloft. The very thought of standing precariously up there on a 'foot rope' sent a shiver down his spine. He earnestly prayed that he wouldn't have to climb up the mast because he knew it must be frightening, especially if the ship was swaying to and fro in bad weather....

"You looking for someone sonny?" a voice asked from behind his back.

He turned around to see Mr Fallowfield looking him up and down.

"Oh, I'm to join the Sea Breeze as a cadet sir but I...."

"Ah yes, I've been told to be on the look-out for you son" said Mr Fallowfield.

"Follow me lad" he added and he led the way up the gang-way and on to the deck of the Sea Breeze.

The lad felt the strange motion of the ship gently swaying which to anyone else would have gone unnoticed. It was quite pleasant but he was reminded of his father's timely but encouraging words.

"You will probably be one of those people who are likely to suffer violent sea-sickness for the first few weeks but you mustn't give up hope there and then son. You will get over it if you persevere"

All eyes turned to look at the young fresh faced, faired haired lad who seemed out of place on the deck of the Sea Breeze. One big black swarthy man with a knife between his teeth stopped what he was doing and watched young Zak follow in the wake of Mr Fallowfield. The gleaming eyes of the man, together with the dirty headband around his forehead frightened him.

"Ah! Boson's mate, this is young Mr Daynty our new cadet. Will you let the Captain know he has arrived safely? I dare say he will want to have a few words with him before he takes up his duties"

"Aye, Aye, Mr Fallowfield, leave him to me" he said and he led the lad aft and down to the Captain's quarters under the after quarter deck.

The lad didn't know what to expect of the captain and he was feeling apprehensive at the forthcoming meeting. The boson's mate led him down the companionway leading to the captain's quarters. He knocked on the door and a deep voice boomed out,

"Come in"

"This is Mr Daynty Sir, the new cadet"

Captain Oakley put his cap on as a matter of habit.

"Very good, I'll take it from here thank you" he said.

Zak was quite surprised to see that the Captain's quarters were quite spacious and furnished to a very high standard. Everything was highly polished mahogany including the curtained windows and the deep window sills. The Captain stood up from his deep red plush chair behind a stoutly built mahogany desk and eyed the lad up and down. He rolled up a number of charts and put them to one side. Zak couldn't quite reconcile the deep voice he had heard with the man's short stature. Oakley couldn't have been much more than five feet tall and was thick set in build but the young cadet recognised the presence of authority in the man's assured composure. Common sense dictated that there must be more to him than size, or lack of it, and young Zak was vigilant to bare this point in mind. Something told him that here was the iron fist sheathed in the proverbial velvet glove.

"I have the letter here from Mr Elias Tallon, dated 3rd February 1883. I understand he is a friend of your father I take it. He tells me that your father, the Reverend Daynty, was very helpful to him and his family during the long illness, and final sad death, of his baby son. Anyway Mr Daynty, out of Mr Tallon's family misfortune has arisen this opportunity for you to pursue a career at sea. Let us hope that 1883 proves to be a telling year in your life. Welcome aboard the Sea Breeze Mr Dainty and I'm sure we can point you in the right direction so that you may fulfil your aspirations to follow a career at sea. In the meantime you will rig your hammock with Midshipman Tom Berry. My first mate, Mr Durkin, will take you in hand when he joins the ship in the morning"

He was about to return to his desk when he peered into Zak's face.

"I don't know whether you are shaving just yet Mr Daynty but I don't encourage my officers to grow beards or moustaches and I'd be obliged if you would bare that in mind….. Thank you Mr Dainty. That will be all"

Zak thanked him and was pleased that the introduction wasn't as frightening as he had anticipated. He left the cabin to find the whereabouts of midshipman, Tom Berry.

He bumped into the second officer, Mr Andretti, in the alleyway who showed him where his berth was. He found himself in a dark cramped cabin deep in the stern and somewhere far below the captain's quarters. He found Tom Berry straining his eyes to read the 'Midshipman's Flag and Bunting Manual' under the mellow light of a flickering oil lamp. The two lads hit it off right away and had lots to talk about. Zak mentioned that he was a bit worried about climbing the mast but Tom told him it was a daunting experience at first but once you got the hang of it there was nothing to it. It sounded easy the way Tom put it but Zak was still very doubtful. They would have continued talking well into the early hours until Tom realised the lateness of the hour.

"I think we'd better turn in Zak because we'll be too tired in the morning and Mr Durkin won't like it" said Tom as if he had gone through a similar experience before.

They turned in but not before they fell into howls of laughter as Zak made several attempts to get into his hammock…. and stay there.

Zak was too excited to sleep and was up very early in the morning feeling a lot more confident. He had talked with Tom into the early hours and learnt something of the ship's routine. Both lads dressed in their uniforms and Zak felt proud now that he was actually on the career ladder. They looked smart under their hats as they made their way up to the quarterdeck. Zak waited nervously near the helm for Mr Durkin to make an appearance before 'eight bells',

Mr Durkin duly emerged from the officer's quarters and ascended the companionway to the quarterdeck.

"Good morning gentlemen" he greeted the boys politely.

"Good morning Sir" they replied in unison.

"My name is Mr Durken and I am the ship's first officer. You Mr Daynty, will take your orders from me unless I decide otherwise. Do you understand?" he said

Durkin turned his eyes to the activity down on the well deck then slowly up towards the forward poop deck in the forecastle.

"Yes sir" replied a nervous Zak Daynty.

There was a long pause as the first officer cast his eyes forward along the deck. The cadet wasn't sure if that was the end of Mr Durkin's instructions and was unsure what he should do next. He managed to catch Tom's eye who indicated that he stayed where he was. Presently, Mr Durkin continued....

"Now Mr Daynty, I want you to work with our agent, Mr Fallowfield, and pay close attention to what he tells you. I will expect you to know all the answers regarding the cargo when we come to discharge it at the various ports in the West Indies"

"Yes Sir" replied Daynty wanting to show willing.

"Report to the cargo warehouse and please convey my compliments to Mr Fallowfield. That will be all Mr Daynty"

Zak found the agent checking cargos against a list on a clipboard and said he had been ordered to report for duty. Mr Fallowfield recognised the lad and handed him the clipboard.

"Well young Mr Daynty, I must say you look quite a dandy in your uniform" he said jovially.

"All these items of cargo must be entered on the official form called 'The Manifest'. It tells port authorities en route what legitimate cargos we are carrying so if it is not on that form it could be classed as contraband"

Mr Fallowfield looked at the lad...

"So far so good, aye! Mr Daynty? We wouldn't want The Sea Breeze to be impounded for smuggling or anything silly like that now would we?"

"Errr... No sir, we wouldn't want anything like that to happen"

"No indeed, so let us do our work once and do it right so that such a situation doesn't arise. Shall we?"

Zak began to appreciate that there was a lot more to this shipping of goods around the world and realised there was a lot to learn. Mr Fallowfield was glad he was able to lighten his own work load as regards the cargoes arriving for the Sea Breeze by handing over some of the responsibility to the young Mr Daynty.

The various items of cargo had already been assigned a specific place in the ships holds by Mr Fallowfield's draughtsmen. This was to ensure an even keel as far as was possible and also to stow it so that the top items were accessible at the first ports of call.

All Zak had to do was to study the draughtsman's drawing and send the cargo to the ship in that order. The last port of call was Falmouth in Jamaica while the first was Port of Spain in Trinidad in the Windward Islands. Of course, he would be expected to know the names of the recipients of the cargos when it came to discharging at their respective destinations.

"After all, we don't want the wrong goods being delivered to the wrong people now do we Mr Daynty?" said Mr Fallowfield.

Daynty soon got the gist of things and was amazed at the variety of cargos waiting to be shipped aboard. There were rolls of carpet and fine drapery, crates of English table china, vases, Sheffield cutlery, Irish linen ware, candles and oil lamps, two well packed phaetons with detached wheels destined for a Mr Thaddeus Markham of Falmouth in Jamaica. Zak couldn't help giving a thought to the horses that would work them and could only assume they had already been sent out on an earlier voyage.

His curiosity brought him back to the rest of the cargo which included two dozen large wood axes, bales of uniforms, several crates of rifles and side-arms, many crates of cannon balls, countless rolls of sail canvas all destined for the naval base at Port Royal in Jamaica. There were building and gardening tools two dozen large bags of Cheshire salt, and even an entire set of house furniture from one of England's best manufacturers. There were several great vats of fine French wines and brandies but the biggest surprise was several tons of Welsh slates and red roof tiles. The strangest was three brass bells lying close to a crate containing two large crucifixes, cases containing two silver chalices, five sets of church vestments, altar linens and other religious paraphernalia with the words expressing the sentiments of the donors, "…..a gift from the faithful". This batch gave Zak hope in that it was evidence to the fact that the word of God was being taken across the seas to the far side of the world. He would certainly tell his father of that when he got back home. He would learn that, in fact, the word of god had reached the Caribbean early in the fourteenth century.

10

He could see that most of the goods were items destined to adorn the great houses of landowners across the Caribbean. With all these fine goods around him it was not surprising that there were pirates roaming the Caribbean….. the selection of booty was endless and too tempting for the greedy. Fortunately for this lot, Tom Berry had assured Zak that the Sea Breeze could out-sail most pirate vessels… given a good following wind.

"Anyway, the Royal Navy do have a presence in the Caribbean so the pirates don't have it all their own way. Not like in the olden days" Tom concluded.

The cargo was being hoisted aboard by using their main yards as cranes and stowed at a fast rate down the hatches. Zak could see the ship visibly settling down in the water as the weight was taken aboard. Before the day was through he had come across further odd parcels of cargo including ten dozen feather mattresses. There was no telling what was going to turn up next. The Blue Peter was hoisted to the top of the main mast to let one and all know that the Sea Breeze would be sailing within the next twenty four hours. Later that afternoon, two ladies and a gentleman, with their luggage, turned up in a coach drawn by four horses. They turned out to be members of the De Witt family going out to their father in St Lucia in the Windward Islands. Mr Durkin welcomed them aboard and took them to see the captain. Their ample luggage was carried to their cabins next to the captain's quarters and it was clear they had plenty of money.

The following afternoon Mr Fallowfield took a sack of mail aboard and left it in the capable hands of Mr Durkin. Then, the water butts were filled under the supervision of the ship's carpenter, colloquially known as Chips, and the hatches were battened down. All sails were made ready to unfurl as soon as the ship was clear of the harbour. Captain Oakley breathed in of the bracing wind that was building up and it promised a speedy start to the voyage.

"Please get into the towing boat Mr Daynty and take note of what is happening about you. The job may well fall to you in foreign harbours so watch carefully" ordered Mr Durkin.

Zack nervously climbed down the Jacob's ladder into the boat. He came face to face with the black swarthy man with the glaring eyes he had first seen with a knife between his teeth when he had first come aboard. It transpired that he was the boson's mate and Zac got the impression that the men were afraid of him.

"Sit on the after thwart in the stern Mr Daynty; you'll be out of harms way there" ordered the black swarthy man.

The lad did as he was told and watched the procedure. The men pulled hard on their oars and the boat pulled forward to the head of the ship. The towing line was dropped down from the bowsprit of Sea Breeze and the boson's mate made it fast.

Captain Oakley stood near the helm on the quarter deck and over-looked the proceedings. The gangway was dragged inboard and Mr Durkin ordered.

"Let go for'rd ......let go aft. Fend off for'ard"

The ropes holding the Sea Breeze to the quayside were hauled inboard and the ship was eased away from the dockside.

"Take her out Mr Turley" Durkin called out to the third officer. The tow boat took the strain as the men began to pull hard on their oars. Presently the ship began to move away from the quay and was slowly eased out into open water. To help her along, Mr Durkin ordered the jibs to be unfurled to help her come around to port. This took some of the pressure off the tow boat and soon the Sea Breeze was in the throws of the wind. The towline was taken up and the tow boat was manoeuvred back to the Jacob's ladder where the sailors, including Mr Daynty, climbed back on board. The tow boat was hauled up out of the water and made fast on the hatch top. Mr Durkin looked about him and when he was quite satisfied all was clear he ordered,

"Hoist the mainsail Boson" and suddenly the canvas was unfurled and could be seen breathing in the stiff wind. Top sails were unreefed from the cross-trees adding further to the expanse of flapping sail and Mr Daynty was very impressed. The sails were trimmed and Mr Durkin ordered the helmsman,

"Steady as she goes"

"Steady as she goes Sir"

Durkin turned to the Captain and asked,

"Should I set a particular course sir?"

"I think we have enough latitude to set a broad course Mr Durkin. Steer a course West, West by South for the Tropic of Cancer. After all, we have a run of some four thousand miles before we are anywhere near our first port of call in the Caribbean"

"Very good sir" replied Mr Durkin then ordered,

"Steer a course West, West by South"

The helmsman had to lean heavily on the wheel to bring the ship's head around on to her new course.

"I think it is safe now to give her all the sail you can muster Mr Durkin" advised the Captain.

The captain took his leave of the quarter deck and returned to his quarters. The second officer, Mr Andretti, appeared from the forward end to take up the eight to twelve watch. After some minutes he rang out 'Eight bells" and the voyage had begun proper.

"Thank you Mr Daynty for your assistance in getting the ship under way and now I want you to accompany Midshipman Berry who will show you how to pay out the log line from the after rail" he said pointing to the stern of the ship and added,

"Mr Berry will explain what he is doing and why. When you have finished I suggest you turn in and get some shut eye before 'turning too' in the morning for the eight to twelve watch. Good night Mr Daynty"

Zack descended to the well deck and turned into the officer's quarters. Tom Berry wasted no time getting into his hammock and began to dose off.

"Well that went all right Tom. Mr Durkin said I am to get some sleep and report on the quarter deck in the morning"

Tom was too tired to start a conversation and advised Zak to do as the mate had told him. Zak lined his hammock with paillasse and tried again and again to get into it. After many failures he was too tired to care and decided to lay the paillasse on the deck and sleep there. He tried hard to drop-off to sleep but his mind was racing.

The ship had gained open waters and she was now swaying from port to starboard. Young Tom Berry was snoring his head off by this time but Zack was beginning to feel wheezy. He thought it was something he had eaten and as he began to think of what it might have been he began to feel dizzy. He called quietly to Tom but the midshipman was in slumber land. In a short while Zak was groaning as his head was dizzy and his stomach was giving him gyp. He felt very ill and thought he was dying. The ship seemed to be swaying precariously from side to side more than it really was and Zak was praying for it to ease off. He asked God for only a little respite for he knew he would feel better but his prayers went unheeded.

His groans became louder and louder until Tom was awakened by the cadets agonising moans.

"What's the matter Zak" asked Tom as he popped his head out of his hammock.

"I'm dying Tom. I'm sure I'm dying. I feel terrible. I know I'm going to die" he groaned

Before Tom could get out of his hammock Zack had spewed up all over the deck. The midshipman had gone through the same experience on his first voyage and knew the feeling. The trouble was that Zak thought he had caught some sort of tropical disease and the thought that it was only seasickness didn't enter his mind.

"You'll feel better if you can make it up to the deck in the cool breeze" Tom said.

The way he was feeling right then he would have climbed the mast to the royal crosstrees if he thought it would make him feel better. Tom helped him up to the swaying companionway but he could hardly stand on his legs. Zak felt as if they were turning to jelly and before he reached the open deck he had spewed up all over the stairway. Tom wanted to get him out of the accommodation area in case the Captain was disturbed. Just as Zak reached the top of the companionway he tripped over the coaming he fell heavily out on to the deck. Just then, the ship heeled to starboard causing the deck to fall away from under his feet. He stumbled to the deck again and with Tom's help he managed to gain his footing and stagger to the ships rail like a drunkard. The coolness of the night was soothing but when he saw the foaming waves swirling past the ship he retched and was sick again. He held on grimly to one of the mast stays and spewed his heart out into the wind. Unfortunately, the contents of his guts were reluctant to leave him as a strong gust of wind blew it back in his face. His legs couldn't hold him up and he began to sink to his knees. Tom urged him to hang on tightly in case a cross-wave swept over the well deck and took him with it. Tom had other business to attend to at that very moment and had to leave Zack to his own devices.

The third mate, Mr Turley, heard the commotion from the quarter deck and looked down to investigate. The truth was apparent and a sadistic streak within him called out to the lad.

"Would you like a nice fatty piece of belly pork to chew on lad? It might make you feel better" he said in mocking sympathy.

The vision of a fatty piece of pork sliding down his throat was too much for the lad and only made him worse. His head was swimming round and round and his eyes were out of focus while his legs were so weak they could hardly support his weight. The foaming sea racing by didn't help and to add further to his discomfort the ship began to pitch and toss.

Everyone knew the lad had to travel the full journey before he would feel better. That was the sort of treatment every seasick victim had received from time immemorial and although there was something psychologically perverse about the treatment it usually had the effect of making the victim fight his way back to good health. However, in Mr Daynty's case, he had only begun his journey and the worst was yet to come. It was in the lap of the Gods as to what terrors he might encounter as he travelled through his first night at sea......

CHAPTER 2

Mr Daynty Finds His Sea Legs

The following morning was heavily overcast when Mr Durkin took the early watch. The ship was running fair and he figured he could get another two knots if he unfurled his top royals and sky-sails to catch the high winds. Midshipman Tom Berry was also on the quarter deck having informed Mr Durkin that Mr Daynty was unlikely to make an appearance due to being sea-sick. The smell of breakfast wafting across the deck from the galley was a welcome distraction for the men on the early watch. Mr Durkin knew that even if he ordered Mr Daynty on deck, the likelihood of him being of any useful assistance was a foregone conclusion. Indeed, Zak was totally incapacitated at that moment and lay down on the deck in his quarters holding his head in his hands. His stomach was far from ready to be fed salt beef but he was on the mend. If only the cabin would stop spinning round and round he felt his head would clear and all would be well. Tom made Zak as comfortable as possible and had already cleaned up after him, especially on the stairway leading from the officer's quarters and on to the deck. He knew the captain and officers would be using it frequently to say nothing of the three passengers.

The boson ordered the top sails to be unfurled and crewmen deftly climbed the shrouds up the ratlines and on to the top yards to undo the reefs with only the foot ropes between them and the deck far below. When the canvas was freed the sails billowed out and caught the wind. As they filled out there was a distinct sense that the ship was moving that much faster as a result. The wind was coming up from the south west and Sea Breeze had to tack to make headway. This would add more mileage and more time to the voyage and time was money in this business.

There was a flurry of activity in the passenger's cabins and things only became clear when the younger lady was shadowed by her older siblings to the heads. There was no doubt that she was as sick as a dog but mercifully, she would be looked after until she was back on her feet. The elder brother and sister took it in turns to take a breath of fresh air on the deck but the girl was kept below deck for the present.

Dawn broke on the fourth day out from Liverpool and the sails were full. Although the sea was choppy, Mr Daynty was feeling a lot better and was gradually finding his sea legs. So much so that he felt it was time to venture out on to the deck. As he emerged from the accommodation he felt the fresh salt breeze on his face and what a refreshing experience it was too, he thought. The sight of the ship under full sail was a sight for sore eyes and he marvelled at man's ingenuity at bringing everything together, the ship, the sails, the wind, the sea and a hearty crew...

Satan, the black tomcat from the crew's quarters, had made him self comfortable and was curled up in a coiled rope on the fo'castle. Everything was running smoothly and each man went about his duties which merely added to the monotony. As the sun came up, the ship was on the port tack and Satan stretched out to absorb the heat of the morning. Suddenly, the silence was broken when a sailor aloft the fore mast called out.

"Ship Ahoy: There on the starboard beam"

Those who were on deck moved aft to the starboard rail and peered westward to the horizon. Captain Oakley was already on the quarter deck taking in the fresh, brisk morning air before going down for breakfast. He trained his telescope along the line of the western horizon.

"What is her course" asked the captain of the second mate. He in turn shouted to the lookout,

"What is her course?"

"She is sailing North, North by East as near as damn it, sir"

She was making good headway because she had the wind behind her. The second mate relayed the essence of the message to the captain. Oakley drew his telescope across the blurred line where the sea merged with the sullen sky. Suddenly he caught a glimpse of what looked like skysails appearing just over the curvature of the earth. Then the rigging became clearer when the royals came into view. In no time at all, he could make her out to be a five mast topsail schooner. He handed the telescope to Mr Ambretti the second mate who looked her over.

"She is sitting low in the water Sir and I suspect she is out from the Carolinas with a cargo of cotton in the hatches and timber as deck cargo. I dare say she is probably bound for Liverpool Captain"

The commotion on deck stirred Satan who decided to make his appearance amidships to Moonbeam's territory. He leisurely stretched his legs then gingerly made his way down the fo'castle companionway on to the well deck. Moonbeam was expecting him and moved forward to confront him. His growls made it clear that he wasn't going to allow Satan to encroach any further into his territory. Both cats stood gesturing at one another with tails erect and anger in their eyes. This demonstration of brevity, on the part of Satan, was a regular occurrence and seldom amounted to anything. He was the oldest of the three ship's tomcats and knew his fighting days were over but he was so used to making his point it had become part of his daily routine. In the event, Satan had satisfied his desire to stand up to the younger Moonbeam then slowly turned away and returned to his own patch on the fo'castle.

The schooner came on relentlessly and Captain Oakley had summoned midshipman Berry to the quarter-deck with his semaphore flags. Make to the schooner…

"Please repeat message" and Tom duly obliged.

The captain handed the telescope to the midshipman to read the reply.

"I.. am.. the schooner.. 'Mary Pellon'… out from Charlston… with.. a.. dis.. place..ment.. of.. 1200.. tons..of.. cotton and.. a deck cargo of timber and.. bound.. for.. Liverpool.."

"Make reply Mr Berry, I am the Sea Breeze out from Liverpool and bound for Trinidad with a general cargo... Thank you Mary Pellon and good sailing" replied Captain Oakley. Tom Berry finished sending the message and when the brief exchange was over Oakley looked at his pocket watch and noted the time purely for purpose of the entry into the log book. The schooner looked a glorious sight under full sail and Mr Daynty couldn't take his eyes off her. The only time he had seen anything like it before was in paintings of the day. Soon, the Mary Pellon got fainter until she disappeared over the north horizon. Sea Breeze returned to normal routine and the Captain went below to the wardroom for breakfast.

Mr Daynty was ordered to accompany Tom Berry to check on and take the midday reading from the log line. Tom explained the readings were taken each day at noon and the ship's progress was logged from noon to noon.

"On this occasion Zak, we have travelled 272 miles since this time yesterday" he said.

"God, that sounds pretty good going Tom"

"Not really Zak. We could have done a lot better with a following wind but with it coming straight at us we have to tack across it to make headway. On a good day we could make 310 or more miles but…."

Zak thought that was fantastic and whistled in surprise. Tom looked at him in horror and Zak wondered what the matter.
was.

"You shouldn't whistle like that Zak especially on deck…you could be inviting stormy weather"

Zak look puzzled and Tom explained that seaman didn't whistle at sea.

"It's a superstition…that's why, and we don't want to invite raging storms now do we? Besides, you might get sea sick again and I don't think you'd like that, would you?"

Sak was reminded of his recent bout of sea sickness and his visit to the threshold of eternity. He certainly didn't want to go down that road again if he could avoid it. Tom spoke in a subdued voice and Zak got the message. That night, he felt the sea held no terrors for him anymore and he slept like a baby.

The next morning he reported for duty on the quarter deck and was greeted by Mr Durkin. The wind had turned several degrees and was now coming from West, West by North. Durkin thought it was time to let the sails out.

"It is nice to see you reporting for duty Mr Daynty and I hope you have got over your …'settling in discomfort'" said Durkin in an understanding tone and a sly smile.

"Thank you sir and all is well. I feel ready for anything now Mr Durkin" replied Zak sounding very hail and hearty.

"Good, good, because you have much to learn and much studying to do Mr Dainty and the sooner you start, the better it will be for you"

Just then, Zak saw the youngest passenger, Miss Anna De Witt, being led out by her elder brother to the ship's rail. She looked a little pale around the gills but other than that she seemed steady on her feet. The officers had been aware that she had been very sick because of the flurry of activity in and out of her quarters by her elder brother and sister.

The latter had sailed down to the Leeward Islands before and had long got used to life on the ocean waves. The sixteen year old Miss Anna wore a long flowery dress to her ankles and a shawl about her shoulders. It was her long blonde hair that caught Zak's attention. It cascaded down her back over the black shawl and Zak had the urge to see her face. Mr Durkin drew Zak's attention aloft to some detail on the skysails but the cadet was determined to keep a weather eye on the girl in case she turned around. Shortly, she did just that as her brother took her by the arm and led her back to her cabin. She glanced up to the quarter deck and caught Zak's eye and smiled. Zak stuck his chest out, gave her a cheeky wink and tipped his hat in recognition then she was gone. This seemingly discreet exchange didn't escape the notice of Mr Durkin but he was worldly enough to turn a blind eye to such spontaneous flirting and said nothing.

Captain Oakley appeared on deck and looked up at the sails.

"With the wind out on the starboard beam, Mr Durkin, don't you think we can come off the tack now?"

"Yes Captain, I was only saying the same thing to Mr Dainty"

Oakley glanced at his cadet and looked aloft.

"Perhaps this is an opportunity for Mr Daynty to acquaint himself with the running gear up there" he said looking aloft but not pressing the issue.

Durkin gave the captain a knowing smile and he too cast his eyes aloft.

"The perfect opportunity I would say Captain"

Oakley took a deep breath and disappeared the way he had come.

The boson had anticipated the probable change to a more direct course and passed in front of the quarter deck.

"I suspect the wind will increase boson so I would be obliged if you will check everything up there before I let the sails out"

"Aye! Aye! sir" he answered then ordered the sailors aloft.

The men came from all angles and scrambled on to the rat lines up to the main yard arms and above. Zak had already guessed that his time had come to test his head for heights and Durkin called to the boson.

"Take Mr Daynty up to the main yard for the present and explain the purpose of the lift, leech-line, bunt-lines, clew-lines, tacks and sheets. That should give him a fundamental understanding of the sail-rigging and an appetite for climbing to the top-gallants and royals at a later date"

"Yes sir" replied the boson as he beckoned to Zak to join him.

"Take good care of him boson, I may require his presence here tomorrow" quipped Durkin dryly.

Zak looked aloft and immediately he was taken by a tinge of fear at the very thought of climbing the rat lines all the way up there. The boson led the lad to the ship's port side and Zak followed him on to the steel 'sheer pole' at the foot of the rigging. Zak looked outboard behind him and saw the sea racing past. What if he fell off the rat lines and into the sea, he thought. Common sense dictated that, if that happened, the ship would be miles away before it could turn about to save him by which time he might well have drowned. He steeled himself and gritted his teeth then gripped the 'rat line' above his head. Nervously, he took his first step towards the 'main yard' that seemed to him to be in the clouds.

"Don't look down Mr Daynty and you should be all right" the boson shouted above a flapping of sail. When he was half way to the main yard arm his grip was becoming so that he couldn't unclench his fists around the 'rat line' for fear of falling. He thought the weather had deteriorated between those few steps up because the mast appeared to be swinging more steeply from side to side. It never occurred to him at the time that the further up the mast one climbed the greater the arc from port to starboard. The boson kept calling to him encouragingly but Zak couldn't help seeing the racing sea far down below out on the starboard side. He was getting closer to the men who were lined out along the yard arm with the only support between them and the deck bellow was the 'foot rope' which was stretched across the sail. Only a few more steps to go now, he thought, and he would be safe on the housing of the lower mast.

The boson was already there and drew the lad's attention from looking down then at an opportune moment hauled him up and across to the mast staging. The sailors cheered as soon as he was safe but Zak was loath to look down towards the deck. He was so petrified that he might fall he gripped the rigging tightly and was rooted to the spot. His immediate concern now was how he was going to get down safely to the deck again. He could see the sailors leaning slightly over the yard-arm leaving their hands free to work the 'reef points' along the 'reef band' and realised it was a matter of distributing one's weight evenly. The boson moved about the rigging with the confidence of an orangutan in a tree and the thought struck Zak that one day he might be able to move just as freely.

The boson was at his side now and he was a great comfort to the young cadet. He pointed out various items of the running rigging and Zak, unknowingly, slackened his grip.

"O K now Mr Daynty, we are going to descend to the deck again. Are you ready?"

Zak just wished to be safely down on deck but he knew he had to do the climbing. Before he realised it his feet were back on the solid steel 'sheer pole' only feet above the deck and he breathed a great sigh of relief. He smiled bravely at the boson who patted him on the back.

"Good lad! You did well! It will be all that much easier next time you have to climb up there Mr Daynty, believe me" he assured Zak.

Sak reported back to the quarter deck and Mr Durkin said,

"Now that wasn't too bad was it Mr Dainty?"

I don't suppose it was, thought Zak, as long as some one else is doing the climbing.

"I have to admit sir that I was a bit scared" he replied.

"You have nothing to be ashamed of Mr Daynty. You did well for your first time and you'll find the more you climb up there the less you'll worry about it"

Zak knew different and wasn't looking forward to his next time scrambling up the 'rat lines'.

Their attention was drawn to the squealing of seagulls soaring and wheeling aloft the masts. They seemed out of place way out there in the middle of the Atlantic Ocean and Zak looked puzzled.

"Its all right Mr Daynty, we are not far away from the Azores somewhere out on our starboard side. You should be able to see the islands anytime now…. assuming there is no mist" he said. After a pause and as an afterthought he went on.

"It might interest you to know Mr Daynty that the Azores are a group of nine islands, volcanic in origin, and are outlying peaks of the Mid Atlantic Range. They have been possessions of Portugal since 1430 and the capital is Ponta Delgada on the island of San Miguel"

The first mate noted the wonder in Zack's expression and after a pause he added,

"I thought that snippet of information would set you thinking Mr Daynty"

Sure enough the islands appeared as black clouds on the starboard side as predicted by Mr Durkin and the three passengers were out to see the sight. Miss Anna De Witt couldn't make out anything resembling an island, as they looked like low dark clouds so the view held little interest for her. However, her attention was drawn to the quarter deck where Zak was feeling like a superman after his epic climb up the main mast. She smiled a broad smile at him that might have said,

"I like you sailor" and that was the message Zak was all too happy to receive.

He filled his lungs with fresh air and stuck his chest out. As with most potential lovers their minds began to contrive ways by which they could make physical contact, albeit accidentally, when touching each other was inevitable.

Someone shouted in delight and pointed far ahead on the starboard beam. Presently several small fishing vessels were visible and one or two were directly ahead in the path of Sea Breeze. Mr Durkin hoped they would move out of his way because if they didn't it meant he would have to alter his sails to get around them. The fishermen waved to Sea Breeze and the passengers waved back. Miss Anna was distracted from eyeing her sailor- boy Zak while he had to stand bye in case the ship had to alter course to get ahead of the fishing boats. The excitement soon passed and Miss Anna turned her attention back to Zak. She became quite bold and now there was nothing subtle about her interest in the young cadet.

At dinner in the wardroom that evening Zak told Tom Berry about his climb up the mast but only to the main beam and admitted how scared he had been. Tom mentioned the young passenger and said,

"I am reliably informed that she has designs on you Zak. The rumour is all over the ship but I'm not sure if it has reached the skipper's ears yet. Is it true?"

"I didn't think it was that obvious Tom. Mind you, I do fancy her but there is no way we could ever be alone on this ship" he said sounding a little disappointed.

"Never mind, I'll show you the rounds as soon as we get ashore in Port of Spain" he re-joined and sounding as if it was a good runner up prize.

"If we keep this rate up that won't be long. After all, we made 315 miles from noon yesterday to noon today" he disclosed.

Zak was about to whistle in surprise when he remembered the superstition.

The following morning the strong wind was amiss and Durkin ordered the main and lower top sails to be 'clewed' up for the present. The sun was hot and the men had shed their heavier outer garments.

"We are almost in the doldrums Mr Daynty" observed Durkin and after a short pause he added,

"The captain won't like it at all. It upsets his entire schedule and adds greatly to the costs of the voyage and cuts into the profits of the ship's owners"

The captain must have been thinking on the same lines because he suddenly emerged from his quarters and strode along the well deck. The main sails and lower top sails were clewed up now and hung limp as the captain looked far ahead to the horizon hoping to see some change in the weather.

"And how are you coming on with your studies Mr Daynty?" asked Durkin in an effort to hold Zak's attention.

"I am studying map and chart projections at the moment sir"

Zak replied hoping Durkin wouldn't spring any difficult questions at him.

"Peters? Azimuthal? Mercator?"

"I'm still reading them in general, rather than in particular terms at the moment sir"

"Well, keep at it Mr Daynty….its always handy to know how to find your way around the world where there are no sign posts, don't you think?"

"Yes sir. Oh indeed sir" replied Zak enthusiastically.

The captain came on to the quarter deck and looked about him.

Durkin could see that he wasn't too happy having lost way due to the weather situation. It could be the calm before the storm he mused……..

The melodious refrain of Ben Ogden's mandolin and Baldy Wades' penny whistle came drifting across the deck from the seamen's quarters. It seemed the perfect accompaniment to the stillness of the weather.

"Good day Mr Durkin….Mr Daynty……. I wonder how long this is going to prevail" said the captain referring to the weather.

"It is not very helpful captain" was all Durkin could think of.

"No it isn't Mr Durkin" said the captain as he went and looked overboard at the sea.

"Let us hope we don't get caught up in the Gulf Stream aye Mr Daynty, else we might get carried all the way back home" he quipped looking at the cadet with a mischievous grin on his face.

The captain looked aloft again and as if talking to himself he repeated Durkin's remark.

"No Mr Durkin, it is not helpful at all" he said and left the quarter deck.

Five sailors had taken advantage of the lull in the weather and had decided to cast their fishing lines over the side. The men took it very seriously as anything they caught was always a welcome addition to their monotonous diet of salt beef. Just then the galley boy, the toothless fifty four year old Mick Brady, appeared on deck with a bucket of swill and proceeded to dump it overboard. The fishermen protested vehemently knowing full well that any fish would ignore their meagre baits and feast on the swill. Brady in defence assured them that it would bring the fish in closer to the ship. By this time Miss Anna De Witt had appeared and was resting her arms on the gunnels. The ship had lost way and was now becalmed in the deep blue water. Brady dumped the swill overboard and waited to see if it drew anything. The swill was washed away by the current but nothing happened.

Then suddenly, Miss Anna screamed with fright as she saw the huge form of a shark rising from the depths and breaking the surface of the water until it was only feet below her. The monster was huge and its great mouth was open revealing rows of sharp menacing teeth. She noted its mean pig eye looking greedily at her before it slid effortlessly back into the sea. Miss Anna was so shocked she fainted and slumped to the deck. Zak also saw the beast and was quickly at her side. She came around almost immediately and pointed to the ship's side. Zak looked overboard and he saw the shark just below the surface of the water. He had never seen such a huge creature before either and was astonished at its size. He turned his attention back to Miss Anna and held her protectively in his arms.

"Now then Miss, you'll be all right now. The creature poses no danger to you now" he whispered as he inhaled the scented air about her.
Her long blonde plaits fell down and he quickly got hold of them. The hair was soft like skeins of silk and she was limp in his arms. She was fully aware of her whereabouts and felt safe in the arms of the young cadet. Then, she looked up into his grey eyes and longed for him to hold her tighter. She wished he would even kiss her but she knew the deck wasn't the place for swooning. He could see that she was over her distress but he purposely held on to her much longer than was really necessary before letting go of her.

"Thank you officer" she said knowing full well that he was only a cadet.

Zak unconsciously stuck his chest out then straightened his hat and advised,
"You should go back to your cabin Miss and take a rest after that frightening experience"
He never let on that it was just as much a shock for him as it was for her. She winked at him and asked if he would accompany her

as far as her cabin door but he declined and reminded her he was still on watch. She took his advice then he returned to the quarter deck carrying with him the sweet aroma of her scented body. It was to tantalise his senses for days to come.

"That was very gallant of you Mr Daynty I must admit" commented Durkin knowing full well that the young lad already had a crush on the girl. Durkin thought Mr Daynty was being led astray by the girl and he feared she might jeopardise his career while he got nothing in return.

"This might be a opportune time for you to climb solo up to the top-sail yard arm Mr Daynty and take advantage of this lull in the weather"

The suggestion hit the lad in the guts but he was intelligent enough to realise that if he had to get to the top of the mast, sooner rather than later, then this was the right time to do it.

"Take your time now Mr Daynty and don't look down and hopefully you'll still be with us when we make landfall".........

CHAPTER 3

Landfall

No sooner had Mr Dainty gained a foothold on the rat lines when he saw the two De Witte ladies emerge from the accommodation and gravitate to the ship's side. He could see that Anna was explaining to her sister what happened when the shark came zooming up out of the sea. They nervously looked overboard then out on to the calm blue sea but other than that there was nothing to hold their attention. Their very presence on deck urged Zak to climb higher but made him feel even more uneasy in case he became 'petrified with fright' and had to call for assistance to get down. He hesitated to take the next step up but his inner pride quickly urged him to climb higher so as to be in a position of safety if and when the ladies happened to spot him. When he was safely on the 'crows nest' he gripped the rigging and dared to look down. Sure enough there was Anna pointing him out to her sister. They were looking up and pointing at him then they began to wave madly. This presented him with a dilemma…. should he take the easy way out and descend to the deck from his present height or should he continue to climb higher knowing that Mr Durkin's eyes were firmly fixed on him.

The very thought of going higher increased his fear and threw up all sorts of doubts and questions as to how he might cope. He realised that, in any event, he would have to climb to the royals, top-sails and even the sky-sails sooner rather than later and now was the time to prove to himself that he could do it and to acquit himself in the eyes of Mr Durkin. He gritted his teeth and hesitantly took a few faltering steps upwards. He persisted as far as the top gallant but any further looked foreboding. He was reminded of one of his father's favourite sayings which gave comfort to his shortcomings,
"Ah my friend, courage in excess is often equated with foolhardiness"

That was a good saying, thought Zack, and not wanting to be foolhardy he instantly made up his mind to climb no further. There was always another day so he descended slowly trying all the time to look confident and carefree in the rigging in the full knowledge that critical eyes were focussed on his every move. As soon as he touched the deck the two girls were there and they applauded his bravery. He smiled nonchalantly as if he had been climbing the masts all his life and the ladies were obviously in awe of his prowess. He saw that Mr Durkin was looking at him so he bid the ladies the time of day and returned to the quarter deck. The remainder of his watch was uneventful and that evening at dinner he related the whole story of Anna fainting and the appearance of the shark to Tom. Tom told him he had already heard the story then he told Zak that the ship would reach Port of Spain within six days providing the wind got up. He then hinted that Zak would have to get a move on if he was to make any progress with Miss DeWitt.

"Your right Tom, she is so soft and tender to touch" he swooned dreamily as he tried to recapture the memory of holding her supple body in his arms. There was hardly any movement of the ship and all was quiet except for the hearty singing of the sailors to the accompaniments of Ben Ogden's mandolin and Baldy Wade's penny whistle. Tom and Zak stayed with their studies for a couple of hours then Zak fell asleep dreaming of Anna, his forbidden love.....

"All hands on deck Mr Dainty. Wake up Mr Dainty, You are wanted on the quarter deck" the voice seemed to be panicking and calling from afar.

"All hands on deck Mr Daynty" the voice repeated while a firm hand was shaking him out of his slumbers. When Zak was fully awake he saw it was the second mate Mr Andretti and there was urgency in his voice.

"What's the matter.....Mr Andretti.....what time is it?"

"It is five bells [3am] and the wind is getting up quite fast" he said as he disappeared from the cabin.

Tom was already on his feet and the two lads went up on deck. The sailors were already aloft and the clew lines were slackened as the limp sails came to life and filled with wind. Captain Oakley was on the quarter deck anxious to get the ship under way.

"Pay the log line out Mr Dainty" ordered the captain as the ship began to move.

Once there was a good spread of sail Sea Breeze was on her way again.

"Steer the same course Mr Andretti… at least until the morning" the captain ordered

The ship answered to the helm and her head came about on course. It was clear that Captain Oakley was greatly relieved, as his eyes were everywhere taking in anything that affected the trim of his ship.

"At least that is a blessing Mr Andretti..... the wind coming from the south east" he said the frustration having clearly left his voice.

28

The lamp trimmer went aloft to refuel the masthead lamps and they were still able to cast a soft mellow glow on the surrounding sea.

Early the next morning Mr Durkin noted a vessel astern heading due north. She had obviously sailed around the Cape of Good Hope on the same wind that had caught up with Sea Breeze the night before. She was deep hulled and was making very good headway. She was too far away for the naked eye but with the aid of his telescope Mr Durkin was able to read the message from her mizzen mast using Marryat's code flags. The message simply declared 'The Marco Polo'. As it so happened, Captain Oakley knew quite a lot about her. She had been built at St John, New Brunswick in Canada only two years earlier and was purchased by James Baines of Liverpool. He had then fitted her out for the booming Australian trade with accommodation for Government emigrants. Oakley had heard that she carried 930 emigrants out to Melbourne, 51 of who were children. He knew her master, Captain James N Forbes, very well because they had sailed together in their younger days. The Marco Polo was 184 feet long with a displacement of 1400 tons in old measure. Oakley knew the date she had left Liverpool and a quick calculation suggested she was making something of a record run from Australia to England. With this first hand information he was able to enter a comprehensive report in the log book…..

Later in the day, the French barquentine, L' Alphonse-Nicolas Cezard of 501 tons, was sighted far ahead crossing the path of Sea Breeze. She was on a course East, East by North and was probably heading back to Bordeaux or Le Havre. She was out from San Francisco on the Californian gold rush route taking out French and other European nationals who's imaginations had been fire by stories of gold for the taking. In such a frame of mind they could think of nothing else but gold, gold, and more gold. The news of the gold rush had infected the minds of all sorts of men and their one aim was to get to the gold fields by any means possible. News had filtered through to the ship owners and maritime communities around the world that many a fine ship that had taken prospectors out to San Francisco was now lying at anchor, unattended, unwanted and derelict. Everyone, including the ship's crews, had been taken with gold rush fever that they deserted their ships and left them to rot. Captain Oakley thought on how the L' Alphonse-Nicholas Cezard had managed to muster a crew for the return voyage but………she was sailing home…… He could only hope that the Sea

Breeze's owners would not be tempted to ply that route for any short term profit......

It was late in the afternoon and the tell-tale signs of landfall had been apparent since that morning. There was a growing increase in small craft criss-crossing the path of Sea Breeze as well as an escort of seagulls. There was a sense of anticipation among the passengers and not least the cadet, Mr Daynty. The first sightings of land, on the run around to Port of Spain, turned out to be small uninhabited islets but they generated a great deal of interest amongst the De Witte siblings. They hugged the ship's side, intent on missing nothing after being so many long days at sea. Mr Durkin ordered 'stand by' and a hundred men appeared. He ordered the royals and topsails to be reefed and the sailors were up the 'rat lines' in no time at all.

With reduced sail, the ship began to lose way and small local bum-boats came alongside and were able to keep pace with Sea Breeze. They offered bananas, mangos, oranges, fresh fish and local fruit juices for sale as well as cocoa nuts, palm mats, straw boaters and new clean paillasses as well as other local products. Far out to port there was a great spread of sail heading West, West by North that turned out to be a Spanish galleon en route to Mexico. Then, as if from nowhere, there appeared the eighty four gun frigate, HMS Culloden, her name a poignant reminder of the great battle of St Vincent and the Royal Navy's victory against the Spanish fleet in 1797.

Durkin, an avid reader of recent naval history, was also reminded of the decisive part Commodore Horatio Nelson played in that decisive victory. Nelson audaciously left his position, third in line, and sailed his ship, HMS Captain of 74 guns, to the head of the Spanish column. He crossed the bows of five large Spanish vessels and then engaged the Santissima Trinidada of one hundred and thirty six guns and the biggest ship afloat at the time. HMS Culloden with other ships in the van joined in. Nelson then joined battle with the San Nicolas of 80 guns and the San Josef with 112 guns while HMS Excellent took on San Ysidro etc and HMS Victory opened fire on the 112 gun San Salvador del Mundo. It was thus, that a comparatively obscure commodore i.e. Horatio Nelson sailed into history. His action made him a national hero while the admiralty rewarded him by promoting him to Rear Admiral. Indeed, it was a younger Nelson who served in the Caribbean squadron prior to St Vincent when he married Mrs Frances Nisbet.…...

Culloden seemed to be on a leisurely cruise and Durkin acknowledged her by dipping the union jack. She in turn responded then both ships went about their business.

"You might well be serving on her a couple years from now Mr Daynty" prompted Durkin knowing that the cadet's presence on Sea Breeze was to grasp the fundamentals of handling a ship under sail.

"We'll have to wait and see Mr Durkin" he replied sounding like a grown up version of the vicar's son who had joined the ship at Liverpool only weeks earlier.

"Who Knows Mr Daynty, you might even turn out to be as famous as Admiral Lord Nelson himself. After all, you do have something in common with the admiral in as much as you both are sons of clergymen" he teased.

Zak thought on Mr Durkin's words and after a pause he replied jokingly'

"Who Knows….Truth is often stranger than fiction Mr Durkin"…

The atmosphere suddenly became hot and clammy and the wind just evaporated and suddenly the heavens' opens up. They were caught up in a tropical rain storm which threw it down like stair rods. Zak had never seen anything like it and he was forcibly reminded of Noah's Arc in the great biblical flood. The ship lost way and Trinidad was in sight. Captain Oakley told Mr Durkin to lower the sea boat and take Sea Breeze in tow. He had lost enough time to date and with his goal in sight the men were just a anxious to make port.

Midshipman Tom Berry was excited at the thought of renewing old liaisons he had forged on his last voyage. He vowed not to drink too much of the local hooch this time knowing how potent it was. The ship moved slowly but she was making headway through the torrential rain. Other sailors were ordered aloft to 'clew up' the sails but in a short time the storm was over and the ship was able to make landfall under reduced sails. Miss Anna appeared on the deck and couldn't resist looking up to the quarter deck. Zak tipped his hat as a gentleman should and she beamed a smile from ear to ear. She was obviously very excited at being so close to land and Zak felt he shared her impatience to get ashore. The ship was sailing west between the islands of Tobago far out on the starboard side and the north coast line of Trinidad out to port. After a couple of hours the ship turned south around the Chaguramas promontory into the gulf of Paria and into the lee of Port of Spain.

The first thing that caught Zak's eye was the lighthouse and close by was the San Andres fort just above the waterfront. Tom had told him that it was built in 1785 to protect the harbour from invaders. Apparently, it had seen a lot of action in its time repelling the French.

"I'll bet that fort could tell some tales if only it could talk" Zak said in a dreamy manner.

"It certainly could Mr Daynty, It has changed hands more than once between the British and the French…but it's ours now"

Mr Durkin drew Zak's attention to another fort a thousand feet up.

"That's Fort George….The signal station"

Zak had to strain his neck to get a good look of the fort but other buildings on the shore line were self evident.

"That is the Roman Catholic Cathedral of The Immaculate Conception built in 1832 and that one there is the Anglican Cathedral of The Holy Trinity consecrated in 1823" said Mr Durkin his arm sweeping along the water line. It began to dawn on Zak that the word of God had taken root here quite a long time ago…..

There was a strong smell of tar and Zak sniffed at the air. He thought someone on board must be working with the stuff.

"Is someone painting with tar Mr Durkin" asked Zak as he sniffed the air.

"Not to my knowledge Mr Daynty but I suspect the smell of tar is coming on the air from the south side of this gulf" he said assuming the lad knew where the stuff actually came from. Zak looked a little puzzled until Durkin explained that the tar was oozing from deep down in the earth and creating what was known as Pitch Lake.

"We might even get a barrel or two and tar the keel when we reach Jamaica if the ship is light" he informed the cadet.

For a moment Zak thought the first mate was pulling his leg about the tar oozing from the earth but he knew Durkin wasn't that sort of person. He took him at his word and could only wonder on this natural phenomenon.

32

Captain Oakley chose his anchorage carefully and Mr Durkin gave the order to 'drop anchor'. Tom Berry and Zak were at the ship's side scanning the golden shoreline when Tom sighed and declared,

"Well Zak, You've finally made your first foreign landfall"........

CHAPTER 4

Island Hopping

The news of the ship's arrival in port had travelled fast through the island and those with any interest in her presence were lined up on the shore waving madly. It was a colourful sight and Mr Daynty was very excited at the prospect of going ashore the following day. His eye was taken by the clear deep blue water of the bay lapping on to golden sands against a background of lush green trees climbing into the hills known as the Northern Range.

There were three other big ships in the bay but it was clear that one of them, the schooner Greyhound, was flying the Blue Peter and was making ready for sea. She was noticeable because of her unique figurehead of a greyhound which was carved in such a way that it appeared to be supporting the bowsprit along its back and had obviously been newly painted.

The three De Witte siblings were standing by for the ship's boat to be lowered into the water to take them ashore. Miss Anna seemed to have forgotten all about Zak as her attention was now focussed on a native gang of labourers working on a new building construction above the shore line. Despite the abolition of slavery throughout the British Empire twenty years earlier in 1833, the white task master stood over them making no attempt to hide the coiled whip in his hand. It seemed that bad practices died hard but Zak was just as fascinated at seeing, what were virtually real live slaves. They were chanting a soulful harmony and if their demeanour was anything to go by it was clear to Zak that the taskmaster wouldn't hesitate to use it. Zak couldn't help noticing that the labourers were not entirely black Africans. They were a mixture of light and dark skins and he only learnt later that some of them originated from such far flung places as Syria and India. They were enticed to come as indentured labourers by the British to augment the labour force left depleted by slaves who had disappeared with the coming of their freedom. He always had a picture in his mind of African warriors covered with war paint, wielding long spears and dancing to war chants.

Half the sailors, numbering about seventy men, were given leave to go ashore but they were warned to be back on board before midnight. They looked a motley of men dressed in an array of loose garb and crowned with a variety of flamboyant head bands and colourful straw boaters. They were obviously bent on seeking out hostelries with good ale and lively wenches who would satisfy their every desire. The De Witte's descended into the boat with Mr Andretti the second mate, followed by 'Chips' the ships carpenter and Hayden Bailey the cook. They were going ashore on ship's business, fresh food stores and herbs, medical aids and fresh water and such like. It was all a matter of price, quality and quantity and both men knew all the tricks of the traders. The traders also knew that to overprice their goods only meant that the ship would take on stores at the next island so the thing was to make a good deal while the opportunity presented itself.

Zak watched the boats run up on the sandy beach and the De Witte's and sailors make a bee line for the interior. Tom Berry asked Zak if he wanted to send a letter home to his family in Cheshire.

"Well, I would if I could get it there" said Zak wide eyed.

"Well then, go and write one quickly and I'll see that it gets aboard the Greyhound which is homeward bound to Bristol. They'll get it into the postal system and it will be delivered to the manse"

"Well, that is very interesting Tom, I'll write a letter now" he replied disbelievingly and hurried off to his cabin.

Other officers, including the captain, also took advantage of this opportunity to get their news home. A bag of letters was duly delivered to the captain of the Greyhound and she set sail early the next morning for the Atlantic. The other ships flagged messages of God's speed and a safe voyage home.

Captain Oakley dressed in his finest outfit under his Panama hat and, when the ship's boat returned he was rowed ashore. There was a horse and carriage waiting to take him to the Governor's house where he was welcomed by the Governor. He delivered two packages which had been entrusted to him by an agent of the government in London. He was wined and dined copiously in the company of some of the more important people on the island.

"I have already entrusted six communications with Captain Arnold of the schooner Greyhound. He is setting sail for Bristol early in the morning" the governor confided.......

They talked on all manner of subjects of 'home' and it was clear that there was a deep interest in the progress of the new Houses of Parliament in London. Captain Oakley was able to tell those present that the building was coming on fine but there were a few years yet before they were finished. The conversation then turned to matters local and the governor touched on points of interest in Port of Spain that Captain Oakley might find interesting.

"If only I had that much time your Excellency" replied Oakley.

Meantime, the able seamen were up the rat lines, rigging the main yard arm in readiness for lifting cargo outboard and lowering it into the native boats which were assembling alongside the ship. Other seamen opened up the main hatch and under the direction of Mr Durken on deck and Zack down the hold, the men began 'slinging' the cargo in readiness for discharging. To save time and costs for the ship owners, all the cargos for Trinidad were discharged in Port of Spain and the respective owners estates.

That night, the sailors returned and it was obvious they had had a fine time. They were carrying bags of local fruit and goat meat and were also carrying three or more of their number who had over indulged in the local tavern. The boson's mate was at the head of the gangway counting the men aboard and there was a lot of laughter and the calling of farewells to a number of local girls who had accompanied the men back to the ship. It wouldn't have been the first time that sailors smuggled girl friends aboard for the night or even to take them to another island....hence the presence of the boson's mate. They partied and sang into the night to the accompaniment of the musicians amongst them.

Early the following day Tom and Zak were excited at the prospect of going ashore "to stretch your legs" as Mr Durkin put it. However, they would have only four hours ashore because they were required to be back on board to take on some cargo and make ready for sea early the next day. As for the other half of the crew, they would get their opportunity to go ashore when the ship made St Georges in Grenada. Zak had glanced at the maps of the islands and it seemed that all the saints in heaven had once descended to the islands many years earlier and staked their claims to their share of them…. for everywhere was called saint this or saint that.

36

Captain Oakley had made the decision to sail within the next 24 hours and Tom was ordered to hoist the Blue Peter before going ashore. As they went down the Jacob's ladder into the boat one of the sailors shouted out to Tom'

"Don't do anything that I wouldn't do Midi"

The boat dropped them off close to the lighthouse and Fort San Andres on the south side of town. The Catholic cathedral was close by and Zak, out of pure curiosity, wanted to go and have a closer look inside but Tom reminded him that they only had less than four hours ashore. Zak was taken by the Red Howler and Weeping Capuchin monkeys that roamed the place at will as well as exotic birds, like the Savannah Hawk and the Red Breasted Blackbird. There was far too much for Zak to take in on this tropical paradise so he resigned himself to be guided by the more experienced Tom.

The fact was that Tom had another agenda on his mind and he was drawn to the native dives in the seedier part of town. He had been wise enough not to have anything of value on his person as he had heard of sailors being set upon and even knifed then left for dead in some dark and lonely side street. They ended up in the Mermaid Inn where Tom had visited on his first voyage. On that occasion everyone had a high old time and he had 'taken Jacqueline upstairs' to satisfy his youthful urges. He fully expected to see her again and to be welcomed with open arms like a returning prodigal son but things had changed. There was no sign of Jacqueline and both lads were eyed furtively as they entered the place by four shifty looking characters sitting at a table in the far corner. At the other side of the room there was a mixed group of people drinking and they seemed to be making merry for some reason. Zak was feeling very uncomfortable and was about to suggest to Tom that they leave when a very big woman waddled over and asked, in flowery musical Carib English.

"Now what can hi get for two young men like you" she asked with a great beaming smile.

Tom was hesitant because he wanted something other than rum. He couldn't remember what he had drunk when last he was there so he stood up and went to the bar. The big woman followed and had to squeeze through the opening to get behind the counter and she pointed out what was on offer. All this time the group of four men were staring at Zack who became unnerved and he was compelled to join Tom. Tom chose two bottles of local beer and the lads supped standing at the bar.

"Hand what ship have you sailed hin hon boys" she asked loudly.

"We are off the clipper Sea Breeze" said Tom politely.

"Mmmm" she hummed and after a pause she added,

"His there henytink else hi can get you?" she smiled and winked mischievously.

Tom guessed there was more to the question than he had first thought and suddenly the truth dawned on him. The woman was offering them other services which might be of interest to two young sailors.

"Err, well err….not at the moment thank you" he replied thinking on his feet.

Just then two much older black buxom women appeared from the back and smiled benevolently at the boys. Zak was getting nervous by this time and felt the situation might get out of hand. The men at the far table were still looking at them and he just wanted to get clear of the place. He knew that he wouldn't know how to handle the situation and was relying heavily on Tom to get them out of the place without any bother. The ladies joined them and Tom saw that they were of hideous proportions. He had his own perception of a comely wench but these two were anything but tempting. If he had fancied them, the normal procedure would have been to offer them a drink and take it from there but Tom said they had to get a move on back to their ship. Tom elbowed Zak, indicating he should sup up. then they made a quick exit into the light of day. Zak let out a sigh of relief to be outside but Tom nodded to two of the men from the bar, who were obviously tailing them. Tom wasn't taking any chances and he began to leg it back towards the cathedral with Zak close on his heels. The two men stayed with them for two hundred yards but the lads were too fast and the pursuers gave up the chase.

"That was a close one Tom" said Zak as they gained the comparative safety of the better part of town.

"It's a good thing we didn't start on the local rum otherwise we couldn't have seen where we were running to" smiled Tom knowing that some of the stuff sold in those low joints was usually so rough and unrefined that it could knock the unwary senseless. They decided to do some sight seeing to pass the little time left but suddenly they were caught up in a tropical rainstorm.

The Roman Catholic cathedral was just ahead and they made a bee line for its open door. Inside, they were approached by a man robed in cassock who introduced himself as Father Ignatius. When they told him they were ashore from the Sea Breeze he volunteered to show them around. It was undeniably a beautiful building and the priest informed them that it was built in 1832....ten years after the Anglican Cathedral in nearby Woodford Square. The building held little interest for Tom who was intent on getting out and making the rendezvous with the ship's sea boat. Outside, they could see the ship's boat waiting just beyond the lighthouse and Fort San Andres. The storm had passed as quickly as it had started and the heat of the day had already dried out their clothes.....

As they climbed the gangway Zak caught sight of Miss Anna talking to her brother. She smiled broadly at him and he was about to doff his hat when he realised he wasn't wearing it. There was too much activity on deck so the two lads went directly to their cabin. During their absence ashore, the ship had taken on 600 large vats of rum and several huge barrels of tar for Liverpool. Captain Oakley did have cargo for Tobago but he was able to broker a deal with a local skipper who agreed to deliver his cargo to Tobago if Oakley agreed to deliver his cargo to Grenada. It was a simply a solution for saving each ship time and money.

Early the next morning the sea boat towed the ship out of the sheltered harbour where she was able to catch what little wind there was. The cook, Haydon Bailey, agreed to cook the piece of meat belonging to Billy Benbow who had been persuaded to buy it when he was drunk. Bailey did his best with the joint but was experienced enough to realise that Benbow had been sold a pig in a poke. When Benbow tried to eat it he found it was as tough as old boots and was obliged to ask his close friend and shipmate, Paddy Ireland, for the loan of his false teeth which they often shared when chewing was tough. Paddy Ireland had the teeth carved out four years earlier from a piece of whale bone by an artisan in Foo Chow when he was on the China tea run. They were cut to suit his gums which had shrunk in the meantime but luckily they suited Billy Benbow much better than they fitted him. Of course, everything had its price and Benbow had to part with a good piece of the meat to Paddy for the use of his whale bone gnashers.

Oakley let the seamen row the ship well out from the shore as Miss Anna went forward to the foc'sle to watch the men rowing the sea boat.

Zak was told to go forward to make sure nobody intruded upon her presence and keep an eye on her. Anna's appearance under the jibs attracted the attention of the men in the boat but the boson's mate tried to keep their attention on towing the ship further out to sea. The sea was translucent blue and presently a 'school' of dolphins surrounded the ship. At first she drew away from the ship's side thinking they were sharks but Zak was able to allay her fears. The boat was hauled aboard and the captain ordered,

"Give her all the sail you can muster, Mr Durkin"

Sea Breeze built up a speed to something like twelve knots and

and Miss Anna watched the dolphins with fascination as they swam just ahead of the ship's bows. They seemed to be playing a game and she invited Zak to join her 'to look at them'.

"Aren't they cute Mr Daynty, the way they leap in and out of the water and keep pace with the ship?" she said hoping to see if Zak would come closer to her.

"They say they are guiding us on our way to the next port Miss"

he replied for the want of something more personal to say.

"You'll be home with your family in a couple of days Miss and I trust you have had an eventful voyage" he said.

"Yes Mr Daynty and I'll certainly miss seeing you up there by the helm" she replied smiling coyly while flashing her eyes and fluttering her eyelashes at him.

He thanked her for the sentiment and stayed with her for over an hour as she watched the dolphins before returning aft to her quarters.

Late in the afternoon, the dolphins were still with the ship as it sailed past Point Salines on the south western tip of Grenada. From that point on Mr Durkin reduced sail by degrees and by the time he was lining the ship up to go alongside the jetty the ship had lost way and the dolphins had gone on their way. The hills rose up steeply out of the water to over two thousand feet in places and there were, what looked like very stout houses, clinging precariously to the hill sides. They all looked as if they had slated or tiled roofs which reminded Mr Daynty that he had stowed several tons of slate and tiles in the holds back in Liverpool for Grenada.

He was to learn later that the town used to be called Port Royale and was destroyed by fire way back in 1771 and 1775 under the French. As a result of such destruction, a law was passed banning the construction of any building not built of either brick or stone and covered with a roof of slate or tiles. In fact, many of the houses were built of bricks brought in by ships as ballast. The Island was passed to the British and the name of the port was changed to St Georges and was known to be the most picturesque town in the Caribbean. Sea Breeze entered the harbour passing Fort George on the left and suitably sited to protect the harbour. Higher up on Richmond Hill, Fort Mathew and Fort Frederick stood sentinel over the views far out to the surrounding sea.

"Well done Mr Durkin. That was very well timed I must admit, I doubt if I could have done it any better" said the captain as Sea Breeze glided neatly alongside the jetty.

Mr Daynty was aghast at another scene that met his eyes. There were two ships lying on their side's way up on a horse shoe shaped beach and his first impression was that they had been physically lifted up out of the water by a giant wave. Although there were men working on their keels he was still under that impression until Mr Durkin explained that the beach in question was called the Carenage where ships were hauled up and laid on their sides, or careened, to use the correct term, in order that repairs may be carried out on the hull. As Mr Durkin put it,

"If the ship is otherwise sea worthy, why spoil her for a hap'ath of tar Mr Daynty?"

Zak was completely taken by the ingenuity of man at the very thought of hauling an entire ship up the beach and then keeling her over on her side, He promised himself to take a closer look at this undertaking when he went ashore.

CHAPTER 5

Mr Daynty Takes The Helm

The next morning the two lads were up early looking forward to their time ashore. Zak had made plans to take a closer look at the careened ships on the beach but Mr Durkin had other plans for him. He told the lad he would be accompanying Mr Andretti to Fort Mathew up Richmond Hill to take an inventory of several tons of equipment packed in crates and containing the personal belongings and effects of the officers and men of the fort. Mr Durkin explained that the government in London had decided to close the fort down for good early the following year and bring the troops home. Zack looked puzzled at the very thought of such a big formidable defence system being abandoned and thought it might encourage the French to invade and take it back again.

"Won't that encourage the French to mount an attempt to try and reoccupy the fort Mr Durkin?" he asked with some concern in his voice.

"That is very unlikely Mr Daynty because the admiralty have assured the government in London that it is well equipped to deal with any such threat from the French, the Spanish the Dutch or any other enterprising brigands, from their naval base at Gros Islet Bay on the Island of St Lucia" informed Durkin.

Zak thought on this news for a moment then asked rhetorically,

"The naval base at where Mr Durkin"

"Gros Islet Bay… just north of here"

Durkin could almost see the wheels going around in the cadet's head so he continued.

"Oh yes Mr Daynty, the English captured the island from the French in 1778 during the American War of Independence. The admiralty then established a naval base at Gros Islet Bay because it was a secure harbour and was protected by Pigeon Island at the entrance. Later on, they heavily fortified Pigeon Island to such an extent that the base was virtually impregnable"

Zak knew there must be more and Mr Durkin went on to explain that there were frequent clashes over the years between the French and English navies but the most decisive battle occurred on the 12 of April 1782 in what became known as the Battle of the Saints. Zak's imagination had been fired and it was clear to Durkin that the lad wanted to know all the details as he knew them. Durkin felt it was his duty to nurture this young aspiring naval officer and instil in him something of the rich and proud heritage of the service. He went on to relate the Battle of the Saints while he had the undivided attention of his student.

"It was called the Battle of the Saints, Mr Daynty, because it was fought off the Isles des Saintes between Guadeloupe and Dominica. The French fleet, at Fort Royal in Martinique, planned to connect with the Spanish fleet at Cap Francoise in Haiti before launching an attack on the English Fort Charles in Jamaica. At that time, Jamaica was under the command of none other than Captain Horatio Nelson. The French believed that a combined French and Spanish attack on Fort Charles, if successful, could rid the Caribbean of the English for ever but things didn't work out quite like that

"The English look-out points on Pigeon Island monitored the French build up at Fort Royal and on the 8th of April, Admiral Rodney received a signal that the French fleet, consisting of more than 150 ships and an army of 10 000 men, had set sail. Within two hours the English fleet was in pursuit. Anxious to avoid a confrontation until they could link up with their Spanish allies the French eluded the English for three days. Alas, the French ships were slowed down on the evening of the 11 of April because of the calmer winds in the lee of Dominica. Then English squadrons, led by Hood, Rodney and Drake closed in and battle was conjoined. The battle raged all day until Admiral de Grasse on his flagship, Ville de Paris, struck his colours in surrender just before sunset"

Zak's imagination could see the broadsides smashing into the enemy and setting them on fire. His vision saw the billowing smoke rising from the doomed enemy vessels while their masts came crashing down on to their decks. He imagined the excitement as the crews of the blazing enemy abandoning their posts and dived into the sea rather than go down with their ships.

He could now see that there was some sense in closing the fort especially if the navy had men of substance like the now legendary Admiral Lord Nelson. His thoughts were brought back to the fate of Fort Mathew.

"It seems a terrible waste of such a grand fort, Mr Durkin"
It was understandable that such a young mind would have a romantic view of a place like the fort but Durkin knew all was not lost.

"There is a strong rumour Mr Daynty that the powers that be in London have decided to turn the fort into the first lunatic asylum in the Caribbean" he paused to see what effect such news would have on the cadet.

"A lunatic asylum!" he exclaimed.

"Are you sure sir?" asked the cadet not quite able to imagine that such a place could ever be anything other than a fort.

Zak thought on the matter for some time and began to realise that such a change of use would entail bringing in doctors, nurses, porters, cooks and a whole assortment of ancillary staff and of course, not forgetting the patients.

"Well why not Mr Daynty. After all, the fort has cisterns that can hold something like 80 000 gallons of fresh water….now that's a good start you must agree" he paused for a reaction then continued.

"There are also kitchens, dormitories, an exercise yard and it even has its own church to say nothing of a stout security wall to keep the patients in. Added to that is the dry moat which surrounds the whole fort…. You could say the place was built with an asylum in mind Mr Daynty"

Zak was going to ask another question but Mr Durkin espied Mr Andretti making his way towards the quarter deck.

"I'm afraid that is the end of the history lesson Mr Daynty. Here comes Mr Andretti. I suggest you go down and collect your clip board, plenty of paper, ink and quills for the task ahead"

Durkin and Andretti chatted for a minute then the latter quickly made his way ashore. Zak was just in time to see him striding along the jetty and had to run to catch up with him. They made their way up the narrow winding road to the fort.

Meantime, the unloading went ahead and later in the day the heavy wooden crates from the fort began to arrive on mules and wagons. Fortunately, Mr Andretti had sent it down in the order it was to be stowed in the hold which helped to save time in double handling. Some of the soldiers made it their business to see their gear was stowed as they wanted but to achieve that they had to unload the cargo destined for Kingstown and stow it on deck to make room. Durkin hadn't argued with that because it made his job that much easier.

The crates came down the hill in a constant stream and were put straight into the hatch. Durkin thought the end was in sight when he saw

Mr Andretti with the cadet approaching the ship later in the day. Andretti reported to the captain while Zack joined Mr Durkin.

"That's a job well done Mr Daynty" he said as the soldiers manhandled the crates into position down the hold.

What do you think of the idea of turning the fort into an asylum now Mr Daynty?"

"You wouldn't guess it from here Mr Durkin but it's a huge place"

Durkin was tempted to say I told you so" but that wasn't his style.

"I'll tell you what though Mr Durkin some of those soldiers have been far too long without the company of females. Some of them displayed the morals of wild animals and only for the presence of Mr Andretti I don't know what might have happened" he said with a note of relief in his voice.

Durkin had a fair idea what the lad was talking about and tried to spare his feelings.

"As bad as that aye Mr Daynty" he said bearing in mind that the lad had spent all of his life in the sheltered confines of the Manse at St Mark's church.

"They reminded me of when we let the cattle out into the fields in the spring back home. They just go wild after being closed in all winter"

Durkin smiled at him then Zak went on.

"Our dioceses used to have a Rev Bertrand Sheald who took over the parish when any of the incumbents were indisposed. He was so effeminate I often thought he used to accentuate his actions but my father told me the poor chap couldn't help himself. The boys in the choir used to call him the 'queer vicar' and treated him like some sort of freak. I must say that whatever his failings, and we all have our share of those, he was always dedicated to the work of the parish and the parishioners"

Durkin was taken by surprise and thought he detected a hint of charity in the lad's voice.

Cargo was still being swung aboard when Miss Anna appeared on the deck. She had obviously washed her hair and now that it was out of plaits it flowed freely down her back making her look even more desirable. Mr Durkin was afraid she might get hit with a sling of cargo so he told Zak to go down, take her by the arm and lead her away from the danger. Zak was by her side in a trice and they stood looking into each others faces for what seemed an eternity. She was scented like a tropical flower and Zak's senses were overwhelmed.

"Mr Durkin has asked me to lead you away from this spot in case you get hurt Miss Anna" he said taking her gently by the arm. He led her forward then across the deck to the water side. She stopped and stooped by Moonbeam, the galley cat, who was snoozing in the sunshine. She tried to stroke him but he didn't appreciate being woke up and he hissed and spat at her with bared teeth and claws at the ready. She withdrew her hand just in time to avoid being scratched.

"The cats are really wild Miss and they don't like being stroked. All they want is to be fed and kept warm in a storm Miss" he said as a comfort.

"They are a bit like me Mr Daynty, except that I like to be stroked" she whispered and smiling mischievously she drew him closer to her side.

A sailor in the rigging called something out to men on the quay and Zak shoved her into an open deck locker believing that something was about to fall from a sling. Suddenly they were close together and out of sight of any one. She was bold and kissed him gently on his lips while their embrace became intimately close. They kissed passionately then Zack realised they might be caught by someone nosing around. They disentangled and he led her back on to the open deck to the ship's side. They looked over the side into the blue water as it lapped against the ship's timbers.

"It won't be the same when you leave us Miss Anna" he said with a touch of sadness in his voice.

The words of Tom Berry came back to mind,

"You'll have to get a move on if you want to take her Zak. She'll soon be leaving the ship and you will have missed your chance" he had said when they were discussing her one night. Zak knew he had passed some chances but here he was close to her once more.

Anna was thinking on similar lines and her mind was scheming.

"Why don't you take me to my cabin now while my brother and sister are ashore?" she whispered and added

"Just for a little while, now that I'm not feeling too well" she said.

Her tantalising invitation was too much to ignore and he knew she would play her part to ensure they were alone. She feigned a headache and was limp in his arms. As he held her closer, her hair brushed against his face causing a tingle to rush through his veins. He sensed Mr Durkin was looking on so he made an open gesture indicating that the girl had a headache and that he was assisting her to her cabin. To his surprise,

Durkin nodded his consent and Zak carried on with renewed hope in his heart. Anna was smart enough not to overdo the act but just enough to justify that Zak stayed at her side. For the benefit of anyone else who might be looking on she laboured her movements as they stepped over the coaming and disappeared into the accommodation. Zak could almost hear Tom, the midshipman, egging him on so he played up to her until they reached her cabin. He feared the captain or one of the officers might suddenly emerge from their cabins and offer to help while the distance to her cabin seemed endless. He needn't have worried about Mr Andretti because he was too engrossed in playing his beloved violin. The strains of Vivaldi echoed into the alleyway which added to Zak's romantic mood.

She opened the door and staggered into the cabin with Zak hanging on to her. No sooner had they entered when Anna kicked the door shut and flicked the dead latch over to lock the door. Zack was going to play it gradually but she wasted no time. She slipped out of the dress effortlessly and to his amazement, he saw that she was stark naked. She kissed him madly and drew close to his body. Suddenly Zak was filled with uncertainty but she made up for that. Before he knew what was happening she had disrobed him and they both fell on to the bed. To be honest, he had never been so close as this to a woman before and everything seemed to be happening at once.

They kissed passionately as they writhed wildly in each others embrace. They turned this way and that across the bed and suddenly she had led him to paradise. They both sighed and their inter-action became still and spiritual. He could have stayed there for life but suddenly he remembered Mr Durkin waiting on the quarter deck. The trouble was he couldn't take his eyes off her beautiful young naked body and he held her close once more. There seemed to be no such thing as time as they looked mistily into each others eyes. His hands were caressing up and down her silken body and he didn't want it ever to stop. She moved sensuously and whispered in his ear,
"I told you I liked being stroked didn't I"
She lightly kissed each of his eyes in turn which only made Zak cling closer to her.

It was Anna who broke the spell as she gently pushed him away.
"I think you had better go back now Zak in case they come looking for you" she whispered.

This brought him back to the pressing business of the moment and he quickly got into his clothes. He was about to leave when Anna put her arms around his neck, kissed him again then straightened his hat. He stepped out of the cabin and up to the quarter deck flushed with having tasted the fruits of Eden for the first time. The scent of Anna danced in his nostrils as he tried to put an innocent expression on his face....

Mr Durkin's eyes were sweeping around the deck taking stock and gauging how long it would take to clear the cargo on the jetty. Zak fully expected him to ask where the hell he had been all that time but the first mate didn't even look at him. He was tempted to break into a chirpy sea shanty but as he was about to blow he suddenly remembered the superstition about whistling on the ship. Through the corner of his eye, Durkin could see that something exciting had happened to the cadet just by noticing the sparkle in his eyes and the renewed spring in the lad's step. Anyone else would have pulled him up but Durkin decided to let sleeping dogs lie...for the present at least. Whatever happened, Durkin was in no doubt that the girl was the instigator and in any case she would be gone for ever within a matter of seventy two hours. About half an hour later Durkin asked, as if it had just occurred to him.

"Oh! by the way Mr Daynty, I meant to ask you how the young lady was when you left her cabin?"

Zak was taken by surprise as the blood rushed to his cheeks. He hesitated before he replied.

"Ah well, I was going to leave right away but she asked if I would stay for a little while until her head cleared"

"And did her head clear Mr Daynty?"

"Errr Oh yes, I think so but it took a little time Sir"

"And she was much better when you left, I take it, Mr Daynty?"

"Oh yes Mr Durkin, I wouldn't have left her alone if she was feeling ill" he replied hoping that Durkin would find his answers matched the questions.

"Well that was a very responsible attitude to adopt in the circumstances Mr Daynty" said Durkin as he secretly admired the lad's diplomatic responses.

Zak felt very satisfied now that he had cleared that tricky point up with Mr Durkin and he proudly filled his lungs with the tropical breeze in the full knowledge that his secret was safe.

Captain Oakley emerged from the accommodation on to the deck and breathed in deeply then made his way to the quarter deck.

"I would like to get her under way before dawn, Mr Durkin, and I'm wondering if you could be ready to sail by then" asked the captain.

The hoisting aboard of the cargo hadn't slackened but the rate it was now coming down the hill from the fort was causing a build up on the jetty. Durkin had to make a mental calculation as to how long it would take before he cleared the jetty but he wasn't sure how much more there was to come down. It was after midnight that the last crate arrived on the jetty and Durkin was able to inform the captain that he expected the ship to be ready for sea around four o'clock in the morning.

"That's good Mr Durkin. By my reckoning, that would mean we could reach Kingstown in the morning… well before eight bells"

"That sounds about right to me Sir" he replied.

The members of the crew were called to their posts just before four o'clock in the morning and Sea Breeze was slowly towed out of the harbour under the light of the swinging oil lamps. Once the sea boat was stowed securely on deck the sails were unfurled. The captain was close by watching to see if there was enough wind to fill the sails but it was apparent it was just about adequate. Perhaps the ship would arrive at Kingstown a little later than first expected but Oakley was satisfied with that.

"Take her out a couple of miles to the lee of the Grenadines Mr Durkin so that we are well clear of the island chain. I don't want to get entangled with the local islanders and their boats criss-crossing my bows for the entire forty miles of the archipelago and I'm in no doubt they will be up and about at first light"

Down in her cabin, Anna became aware of the curtains surrounding her bed gently swaying and, together with the creaking timbers; she guessed the ship was under way. Mr Daynty was on the forward poop overseeing men adjusting the three jibs on the bowsprit. The ship had gathered way and unsurprisingly, the dolphins had already taken up their positions around the bow as it cut through the water. Once the jibs were set Zack began to make his way aft to the quarter deck when he saw Anna coming towards him. His heart began to beat fast with excitement as she drew closer.

"Its too hot in the cabin Mr Daynty so I thought I'd come and see the dolphins again" she said hoping it sounded like a good excuse to get closer to her lover.

"I wouldn't hang too far over the side if I were you Miss Anna in case you topple over the side into the water"

She smiled.

"What if I did fall into the water Mr Daynty? Wouldn't you dive in and save me?" she said taunting him with her smile.

"Nobody would know you had fallen overboard Miss"

"Well then, you will have to get permission from the officer to look after me, now won't you Mr Daynty?" she said knowing that if push came to shove she would win the day.

Zak mentioned Anna's intention to Durkin who knew where his duty lay.

"I think you should stand by as long as she is up there" he said referring to the poop deck.

"Very good Sir, I'll keep an eye on her and see that she doesn't do anything silly" replied Zak, his heart pounding at the very thought of being close to her again.

They watched the dolphins for an hour then spent the time talking of their pleasurable exploits in her cabin. It was all he could do to keep his hands off her but he knew that would be pushing his luck. As time went on, he could see that she was tiring so he tried to persuade her to go to her bed and rest. As the eastern sky began to lighten with the coming dawn he spotted a pod of hump back whales far out on the port quarter. They were travelling east towards the Atlantic and the colder northern climes.

"Look! Look Anna, over there" he pointed far out to port.

Suddenly she was wide awake as she followed his pointing finger.

"There. Humpback whales, they are returning to the north Atlantic with their new babies" he told her.

By the time she caught sight of them they had just dived under the sea again but she was touched by his mention of the mothers and their babies. She had never seen whales in the wild before but had heard people talk about them when the whaling ships had returned to England with their catch.

The animals surfaced again and Anna was thrilled to see them and the young ones swimming along, unconcerned about anything else around them. Presently they had disappeared through the St Vincent Passage into the growing daylight and now it was Zack who was feeling tired. Anna agreed to go to her cabin for a lie down which was a great relief to Zack who returned to the quarter deck. Durkin handed him the telescope and asked him to keep a sharp look-out to the port side. He fully expected to see the island of St Vincent coming into view at any moment.

A voice in the rigging shouted,

"Land on the starboard quarter, Land on the starboard quarter" and Zak trained his tired eye on the horizon.

"He's right Sir" said Zak, as he caught sight of Fort Charlotte high up on Berkshire Hill and overlooking the entrance to Kingstown harbour. Since making the West Indies he had become used to seeing fort this or fort that all over the place and it seemed that St Vincent would follow the trend.

He handed the telescope to Durkin for confirmation who gave the order to reduce sail. Having already discussed with the captain to allow the cadet to take the helm, he ordered Zak to take over from the helmsman. As he took control of the wheel he gritted his teeth and bit his lower lip in the hope that all would go well. Durkin kept a close eye on the run-in and Sea Breeze lost further way as she glided silently past Battery Hill and into the safety of Kingston harbour.

CHAPTER 6

Farewell Miss Anna

Zak had taken the wheel three or four times before while out at sea but that were only to get the feel of how the ship responded to the helm. The ship would veer off course constantly because of waves or wind and it was the helmsman's job to bring her back on course. There was plenty of room for mistakes out at sea for the learner simply because there was all the time in the world to correct any errors but steering the ship alongside a quay was a different matter altogether. One had to exercise judgement regarding the distance and speed to avoid crashing into the wharf. Durkin had gauged the reduction in sails and had to oversee Zak's movements.

"To port" Mr Dainty, "Easy now, easy, steady as she goes" he advised as the ship approached Grenadines Wharf.

Zak caught on to the fact that the rudder was slower to respond to the action of the helmsman when the ship was barely moving and that meant he had to think ahead and take action slightly beforehand. Sea Breeze came alongside Grenadines Wharf with a slight bump but any overshoot was arrested by the immediate restraint of the mooring ropes.

"Well done Mr Dainty" a voice said from behind.

It turned out to be Captain Oakley who had watched the entire operation. Zak turned around and Oakley smiled amiably and nodded with satisfaction. Mr Andretti, the second mate, then   inspected the mooring ropes and, satisfied all was secure, ordered the gangway to be pushed out on to the jetty.

By this time the sun was up showing that the harbour had a unique natural charm of its own. There were warehouses on the wharf which, Zak later discovered, were built of bricks brought in as ballast from England. The bricks were then discharged to make room for cash cargoes such as Molasses and sugar. One of the buildings was the Arrowroot Warehouse that was on the ship's cook's itinerary. This was because ship's cooks would stock up with the stuff and eventually mix it with ground chalk and other 'secret' ingredients to administer to members of the crew who suffered from stomach trouble such as ulcers. It never took up much space in the galley but it brought in extra income for the cook or exchanges of value when there was no where else to go to relieve the pain.

It was only then that Zak saw Miss Anna and her older sister who had watched him steering the ship into harbour and finally alongside the wharf. Anna was all smiles as Zak made his way down the companionway to the well deck. He didn't want to appear too intimate with Anna, at least, not in front of her sister and knowing full well the captain was probably looking on. The main yardarms were being made ready to discharge the cargo some of which was already stacked on deck.

"I think you ought to get clear of the yards for your own safety ladies" said Zak authoritatively and pointing up to the mast.

The ladies saw the danger and retired back to their cabins where they continued to pack their luggage. They would be leaving the ship some time the following evening when the ship was due to arrive at Gros Islet on the north western tip of St Lucia, some thirty miles north east by north of St Vincent.

Mr Andretti was supervising the discharging of the cargo and presently he saw a priest clad in a white robe standing at the foot of the gangway. The man was obviously waiting to see somebody so Andretti went down the gangway to meet him.

"Good afternoon Sir" he greeted the priest.

"I am Father Joseph McArdle and I have come down to take charge of the church bells and vestments for St Mary's Roman Catholic Cathedral" he said, pointing up the shore towards the church.

"Ah yes, that consignment will be discharged in about two hours from now sir" he informed the priest.

"By the way, my name is Andretti…. and I am the second officer on Sea Breeze" he offered his hand and the priest shook it warmly.

Andretti was looking up at the church but couldn't see any steeple and wondered why it would want bells when it didn't even have any apparent place to hang them, He mentioned this fact to the priest who went on to explain.

"Ah yes, and how observant of you Mr Andretti. Indeed you are quite right. The truth of the matter is that the plans have been underway for some time to build the tower and also a proper sanctuary but….." he raised his hands high and sighed resignedly,

"…. but unfortunately the funds Mr Andretti, the funds have not been forthcoming as promised"

Andretti sympathised with the church's dilemma and by way of compensation he concluded,

"Well anyway Father these bells are a good start Aye?" he said and as he was about to return aboard the ship he reminded the priest,

"You know of course that they are quite heavy Father. In fact, one weighs thirteen hundredweight and the other one is eleven and a half hundredweight"

"Well thank you Mr Andretti for that information. In that case, I'll just nip up to the Cobblestone Inn and have a word with the proprietor, Patrick O'Dowd. He is well qualified to take charge of loading the bells on to the carts which should be here presently. You might find time to have a word with him, Mr Andretti, as he was a seaman about ten years ago. You will find him a very interesting and knowledgeable character into the bargain"

"I might just do that Father" he replied.

He climbed back aboard the ship and the priest headed for the Cobblestone Inn.

Andretti was discharging the cargo when a burly thick set, red haired man in his late forties, came running down to the wharf. He was dripping with sweat and he turned out to be O'Dowd. He was relieved to see that the bells had not yet been unloaded and mopping his brow he called to Mr Andretti aboard the ship.

"Permission to come aboard Mr Andretti"

Andretti beckoned him on and O'Dowd introduced himself.

"What can I do for you Mr O'Down?"

"Father McArdle has explained about the bells, Sur, and I came down to ask if you would keep them aboard until the carts arrive to take them up to the cathedral. It will save us a lot of trouble, so it would, if you would land them straight on to the carts" he explained.

Andretti could see the point he was making and was about to ask how long the carts would be in coming when suddenly they appeared approaching the ship.

"Ah sure, tork of the divil himself, Mr Andretti, why here they come" he said, not having lost any of his Irish lilt.

The carts were accompanied by several local black men whom O'Dowd explained airily were '....members of the congregation to be sure....' He went on,

"Sure I'll be organising the landing of the bells on to the carts now Sur" he said taking his leave and going ashore.

O'Dowd could see that the bells were easier to handle once they were hanging from the yard arm and could pose a problem if he had to lift them straight off the ground. The second mate had his doubts as to whether the carts, which looked quite rickety to him, could take the weight but he needn't have worried. They turned out to be very sturdy against all the odds and well capable of taking their weight. O'Dowd hadn't forgotten the unloading procedure and within two hours the bells, together with the crate of vestments, the large crucifix and the rest of the church paraphernalia were hauled up the cobbled streets to the cathedral and unloaded without incident. O'Dowd had invited Andretti and friends to his establishment for that night and never one for refusing an opportunity to sup and dine away from the ship's monotonous diet of salt beef and stale bread, he had gladly accepted.

That evening, Andretti and Durkin made their way up to the Inn and they had taken cadet Zack and midshipman Tom Berry along as a reward for their good progress with their studies. O'Dowd had heard that Mr Andretti was an accomplished violin player and had invited him to bring his instrument along with him. During the meal O'Dowd told them that the Cobblestone Inn was built of ballast bricks from England and that he had bought it with a deposit of gold from his 'prospecting' days in California while the remainder would come out of his future profits. The trouble at first was, he admitted, that he had something of a drink problem and his profits didn't see the light of day. It wasn't that he didn't have the customers or anything like that. They patronised his Inn because he, being an accomplished honky tonk pianist, would entertain them into the early hours with all the sea shanties of the day.

The trouble was that the more he played the more customers sent drinks over to him. By the time he came to close the place in the early hours he was hardly able to make his way to his bed. When he sobered up he would find that his staff had pilfered money from the cash drawer but nobody ever owned up. It was one of the clergy from the cathedral who had taken him in hand and brought him up against the buffers of real life. With the latter's help, he learnt how to conduct his business profitably and within eighteen months he was in the black and he had got more control over his drinking. The following year, he had given up drinking alcohol altogether and was able to get his life and the business on a sound financial footing.

The conversation then came around to the three De Witte siblings which brought a glint to O'Dowd's eye.

"Ah yes, Al De Witte. Now there's a man who owes all his wealth to his grandfather Captain Algernon De Witt who used to terrorise the Caribbean in the 1780s with his band of brigands on his ship, the brigantine Buxom Lady. He acquired his wealth by plundering any vessel, French, Dutch and Spanish, that he thought would be carrying interesting cargos and especially gold. He was forced to retire from the sea when his eyesight began to fail due to, so the story goes….." he lowered his voice at this point

"…. due to syphilis. Apparently he couldn't control his sexual urges and desires and the abduction of women who took his fancy was all part of his lecherous lifestyle. He was once pursued by two French ships after sinking one of theirs and taking two of their high society women prisoner into the bargain. The French had chased him relentlessly but he gave them the slip and found sanctuary at an inlet at Lowvet Point in St Lucia. He felt quite secure there and decided it would be the ideal spot to set up his retirement. Indeed, he went on to entertain his old pirate friends for quite some time until he died five years later.

His son of the same name made a mint out of slave trading as a broker and continued to develop the estate until he died. His son, the present owner and the father of your passengers continued right up to 1807 when the slave trade was outlawed in the British Empire. Then came the abolition of slavery in 1833 when he was supposed to set them free but, people like the De Witts, held on to most of them to work the plantations…. and that gentlemen, is a potted history of the De Witts' of Lowvet Point up to and including your passengers…….

O'Dowd fated his guests with drooling roast chicken accompanied with all kinds of tropical vegetables and fruit. He had played the piano for them and was accompanied by Mr Andretti on his beloved violin. The latter had played a couple of his favourite Vivaldi pieces that went down with great satisfaction with all those present. By the time they left to go back to the ship they knew they had eaten a memorable meal….

Back on the ship that night, Tom and Zak mulled over their invitation to O'Dowd's place and talked at length about the meal then on to the lurid history of Anna's forbears.

"Who'd have thought she was the great granddaughter of a notorious pirate Zak" said Tom still moved by the revelation.

"Yes, I must admit I got quite a shock when O'Dowd told us"

"Did she ever mention anything about her family's connection with piracy and slave trading Zak?"

"No never. Maybe her parents haven't told the children about great granddad Algernon. I mean, it isn't very nice to learn that your great grandfather died of syphilis" explained Zak.

"I dare say the story is part of the De Witt legend and is known all around the Caribbean" Tom suggested.

"With such an antecedence, I find her even more attractive… like finding out that your mother is the daughter of a gypsy king or something of that nature. There is a certain romance about it all don't you think Tom?" said Zak as he wondered about the many hidden possibilities…….

The three De Witts were very excited at the thought of seeing their father again. So much so that their travelling trunks were packed and stacked on deck ready for going ashore on their arrival at Gros Islet. When everything was made secure for putting out to sea, a horseman arrived on the Quay. The rider dismounted and hurried up the gangway and asked for the captain. He was shown to Oakley's quarters where he introduced himself as Mr Frederick Semple from the St Vincent Botanical Gardens.

"And how can I be of service to you Mr Semple" asked the captain.

"I have a package of rare plants and seeds on my horse for the Royal Botanic Gardens at Kew in England and I wondered if you would be so kind and take them along with you" he said.

The captain had heard of the work carried out at Kew Gardens and was only too willing to be of assistance.

"How big is your package Mr Semple?" he asked just to be on the safe side.

Semple indicated the height etc and seeing it was more or less hand baggage, Oakley agreed. Semple went ashore for the plants and brought them aboard. Captain Oakley was suddenly interested in Semple's work and couldn't resist asking questions.

"Why can't Kew grow their own plants Mr Semple?"

"Well Captain, you might be surprised to know the St Vincent Botanical Gardens are the oldest in the western hemisphere and was founded in 1765. Indeed, we have been supplying rare seeds and plants to Kew ever since" he said

"I would never have guessed that Mr Semple. Mind you, I must admit that this is the first time I have sailed this part of the world so I would ask that you bear with my ignorance on this point"

"I quite understand Captain" he said then went on to explain.

"You might be interested to know sir that we also have bread fruit trees which were brought here from the Pacific by Captain Bligh on HMS Providence in 1793 so you can see, that a lot of the rare plants you enjoy in England owe a great deal to men like your good self"

Oakley was secretly flattered to be associated with the name of Captain Bligh and he agreed to take them to England. He could see the man wanted to be on his way so he walked him to the gangway. Semple's parting words were,

"They will keep best in a cool, dry, dark position captain"

Oakley had been so fascinated with their talk that he gave his word that he would personally take special care of them.

Semple mounted his horse waved goodbye and rode off.

Some of the crew went ashore that night and some of them returned the worse for drink. One man, Sam Meadows, had bought a St Vincent parrot, a breed which was becoming rarer and rarer. He had promised his young son that he would bring a parrot home for him if he could find one. Needless to say, Sam spent a lot of time talking to it and became very fond of the creature. He had decided to hang on to it mainly because he was worried it would bite his son as he had learnt to his own cost. He would tell the boy he had forgotten about it but would promise to get one next time.

Early the following day Sea Breeze was shadowing the west coast of St Lucia as she headed north to the naval base at Gros Islet Bay. As the ship was abreast of Soufriere, half way along the coast, there was a lot of local activity in and out of the port that focussed Zak's attention. Anna was feeling the end of the voyage more than her siblings. She longed to spend a little time with Zak before it was too late but he had been ordered to take the helm. It was another glorious day and Anna was on deck hoping he might come down from the quarter deck to be close to her.

Zak eased the helm further to port to get closer to the coast on the run up to Rodney Bay and the naval base at the top end of the island. He was secretly anxious to see the place from where the English fleet had set out to defeat the French in the 'Battle of the Saints' back in 1782. As he steered the ship further to port, Durkin pointed out Pigeon Island at the northern tip of Rodney Bay on his port side.

"There's our old friend again Mr Daynty, HMS Culloden" said Durkin pointing towards Pigeon Island and somewhat surprised at seeing Culloden for a second time. There was a brigantine standing off from the frigate which turned out to be the French merchantman 'Mystere'. She had come under suspicion, north of Martinique, of being engaged in piracy and was arrested and boarded by marines from Cullodin. The captain of Mystere had vehemently protested his innocence but his pleas didn't cut the mustard with Captain Emsley. He had been ordered to be on the lookout for the missing English schooner 'Mirabelle' which seemed to have disappeared from the face of the earth. She had been sighted several times heading for Jamaica but she didn't arrive.

When Emsley had first sighted the Mystere she had immediately changed course away from HMS Cullodin that raised his suspicions. He gave chase and on the following day when he caught up with the suspect north of Martinique he fired a warning shot across her bows. To Emsley's surprise, Mystere had then uncovered hidden cannon and opened fire at close quarters on Cullodin. Although taken by surprise and slightly damaged, HMS Cullodin outgunned the Frenchy who, seeing the writing on the wall, hoisted the flag of surrender. Emsley put his marines aboard and upon inspection he found that her cargo of tea and rolls of silk didn't tally with her log book and ship's papers. Emsley decided to take the ship into custody and escorted her back to Gros Island Bay where further investigations were pending. For one thing, Mystere would have had to have been on the China run to have picked up such a cargo but Emsley's intelligence was that Mystere had been roaming the Caribbean aimlessly for quite a long time….and probably waiting for a victim…… There was a heavy suspicion that the French captain had stripped Mirabelle of anything that was useful to him then scuttled her to hide his crime…….He would have felt quite safe in Martinique since it was at Troisilets in the south west that Marie Josephe de la Pagerie was born on her father's plantation …and later became the wife of Napoleon Bonaparte…….

"If I remember correctly Mr Durkin most of that cheese down the main hold is for the naval base and I wouldn't be surprised if Culloden is waiting to get her share of the stuff" said Zak by way of a light hearted quip while not realising how close he was to the truth.

"I'll be glad to see the back of the stuff Mr Daynty. The tropical heat is beginning to get at it and the smell down the hold is becoming a bit whiffy" said Durkin....

Sea Breeze was well into Rodney Bay and heading further inshore.

"I think its time I took the wheel Mr Daynty as this requires some tricky manoeuvring" said Durkin as Sea Breeze straightened up to sail through the jaws of Gros Islet Bay.

"Oh! Mr Durkin, I'm sure I can take her in without mishap" said Zak almost sounding like a plea.

Mr Durkin had to think hard on the lad's request as he had the ship's safety to bear in mind. He had to make up his mind quickly because it was almost time to turn hard to starboard. He decided to put the lad to the test....

The ship was fast heading for the jaws of the inlet and the time was now or never to come to a decision.

"Very well Mr Daynty. Stand by" Durkin ordered.

The expression on Zack's face changed to one of satisfaction and as was his habit, he bit his lip with determination.

Sea Breeze glided through the jaws of the inlet and Zak waited for his next order.

"Hard a' starboard Mr Daynty"

"Hard a' starboard it is sir" the cadet confirmed confidently and the ship turned sharply right.

It had to go some distance before turning slowly around in a left handed horseshoe manoeuvre so as to come back towards the quay... starboard side on. Zak felt the tension and excitement rising in his veins at being at the helm and he turned it this way and that to keep her on a strict course to come alongside the quay. The ship seemed a little fast but Mr Andretti was on hand to get the mooring lines ashore and made fast in time to arrest the ship's momentum. As things turned out it was a text book docking and Mr Durkin gave the lad credit for his quick thinking and his dexterous handling of the vessel.

The De Witts were hanging over the gunwales trying to see if their father was waiting for them but there was no sign of him anywhere. His absence was clearly a disappointment and a looming anti climax to their long voyage from England. As soon as the gangway was put out on to the quay Anna's brother hurried ashore. He looked up and down but still there was no sign of his father. It certainly left the sibling's expectations deflated leaving them unsure as to what they should do next.

Meantime, the rigging was being made ready for discharging cargo for Gros Islet Bay, including the remainder of the crated cheeses. It had been arranged by the ship's agent to tranship smaller cargoes destined for outlying Leeward Islands such as Antigua, St Christopher, Barbuda and others. This saved Captain Oakley several days in time while leaving Sea Breeze a free run to Port Royal in Jamaica. More barrels of rum and molasses arrived on the quayside together with one hundred and sixty tons of brown sugar and two hundred or more hogsheads of tobacco destined for Liverpool. Fortunately, the hogsheads were a standard three foot six inches high so as to fit comfortably in the Liverpool tobacco warehouse whose floors were just able to neatly accommodate them two high. They stowed neatly into the bottom of the hold and acted like ballast upon which other cargo could be stowed securely.

A couple of hours later a voice from aloft called to Mr Durkin and pointed to a boat coming alongside the ship. Upon investigation, Durkin saw it was a standing lug cutter named the Martha De Witt and he guessed the man on board was the sibling's father. Durkin drew its presence to the attention of the siblings who ran across the deck to the port side. There were shouts of delight as father and children set eyes on each other in a long time.

Zak watched Anna but she didn't seem to relish the thought of leaving the ship. Mr Andretti had ordered their packing cases to be lowered straight on to the deck of the cutter while Zak rolled out the Jacob's ladder down to the cutter. The son was on the deck of the cutter in a jiffy followed by the eldest sister then it was Anna's turn. She seemed unsure as what she should do next and her eyes fixed on to Zak's. They looked deep into each others eyes for what seemed an eternity as they relived that moment of shared ecstasy in her cabin. She saw the sadness in Zak's eyes and they both realised that this would be the last time they would see each other.

"Anna, Anna," an impatient voice called from the cutter and Zak took her gently by the arm and turned her round towards the Jacob's ladder.

Tears began to stream down her cheeks and he gently wiped them away with his handkerchief. He so desperately wanted to take her again in his arms but that would have been presumptive and would have looked like he was taking liberties. The voice called her name again and she knew it was time to say goodbye. She held Zak by his arms and boldly kissed him on the lips. He found her very touch a scintillating and tingling experience as they let go of each other and she quickly descended into the family cutter. Her brother and sister went into the cabin with their father while the native crew hoisted the sail and headed out of the inlet. Zak stood waving forlornly and without moving his lips he kept repeating,

"Farewell my lovely, Farewell Miss Anna" while she remained on the deck of the cutter holding on to the stern rail.

He could see tropical storm clouds gathering way out to sea and knew the cutter was sailing around the north of the island then south to the De Witt's estate which was situated inland from Lowvet Point on the east coast. The cutter became smaller and smaller and as he watched her disappear into Rodney Bay he felt a part of him went with her. For the last time he waved and whispered,

"Farewell Miss Anna" and then the boat was gone. Anna, his first love was gone…. and gone for ever.

Late the following afternoon Sea Breeze set sail for Port Royal in Jamaica and everything was battened down for the crossing. As the island of St Lucia receded astern he whispered yet again,

"Farewell Miss Anna, Farewell my lovely" and a telling chapter in his young life was over.

CHAPTER 7

A Stormy Setback

Durkin set a westerly course and for the first day the ship made good headway. Mr Dainty took the reading from the log line and was surprised to learn the ship had travelled three hundred and seventeen miles which worked out at an average speed of thirteen knots.

"If we can keep this rate up we might reach Port Royal within the next two and a half days Mr Daynty" Durkin informed him.

The captain made his way up to the quarter deck and seemed to be deep in thought. He looked all about him then up the masts and at the sails but Durkin thought he looked troubled. Oakley shook his head and went over to Mr Durkin.

"Everything seems in order but I fear my barometer must be playing up. The readings seem to belie the prevailing conditions Mr Durkin" he said looking a trifle puzzled.

Durkin couldn't suggest anything other than tap it, to wake the mercury up so to speak, because, as far as he was concerned, everything seemed set fair with a good following wind. The captain looked about him again then left the quarter deck. Durkin could see that the man was ill at ease as he made his way forward pausing at intervals and eyeing this or that piece of tackle at close quarters. As far as Durkin was concerned the ship was sailing fair and seemed to be chasing fleeting storm-clouds to the west.

There were several sightings of ships in this wide expansive part of the Caribbean that surprised both Oakley and Mr Durkin. Ships crossed from the Lesser Antilles in the south to Hispania and Cuba in the north and from Barbados in the east to Mexico in the west. There was even a small fleet of vessels, surrounded by their harpoon boats, which were probably on the lookout for migrating whales. Alas, there was a notable absence of sea birds over them, which seemed to suggest that they had a lot more waiting to do. Early on the fourth morning Durkin reckoned that Jamaica was only three hours due west and he corrected his course for Port Royal. Among the comings and goings of ships, it wasn't surprising for Sea Breeze to cross paths with the Royal Navy in the guise of HMS Ardent and HMS Venerable. Just the sight of them suggested they were in the realms of safety, law and order.

Before dawn, the Blue Mountains on the south east of Jamaica loomed huge and black to over 6000 feet against the dark western sky. The boson and sailors were already aloft the forward mast, rigging the yard arm for unloading the cargo. As the sun rose in the east the mist on Blue Mountain quietly surrendered to the new day and the golden hue of dawn tinted the cloud layers down to sea level. When the coastal outline became clearer Durkin was able to identify Morant Point on the south west tip of the island. He set a course knowing that it was then only a case of following the coastline for fifty miles to Port Royal.

He kept scanning the coastline for further identifiable land marks until he spotted the Palisadoes straight ahead. The Palisadoes was a lick of land jutting out from the mainland and enclosing Kingston Harbour. On the open sea side of the Palisadoes was the Port Royal naval base where, Durkin informed Mr Daynty, Captain Horatio Nelson served as the Post Commander some seventy years earlier from 1779 to 1780. Further along to the end of the spit was Fort Charles. It was built in 1655 as a key battery in the island's fortifications and guarded the entrance to Kingston Harbour behind Lime Cay. So popular was Nelson at the time that the fort ramparts were known as Nelson's quarter deck.

Durkin had already started to reduce sail as Sea Breeze sailed past Port Royal towards Fort Charles. There were two more naval vessels in Port Royal and beyond, across the Cay, one could see the masts of several merchantmen reaching for the sky in Kingston Harbour. It was time to stand-by to enter port and Zak was on hand to take the helm. As they reached Fort Charles on the port side a ship under full sail could be seen heading out of the harbour. Mr Durkin took the helm anticipating that, with the two ships converging on the entrance to the harbour, he could expect some tricky manoeuvring as they approached each other.

The ship coming out turned out to be the Portuguese topsail schooner, Elimo Delveria, bound for Recife and Rio De Janeiro in Brazil. Her captain seemed to be more concerned with making a point of her bigger size and perceived importance as his ship loomed down on Sea Breeze. As the distance closed between them Sea Breeze was edged dangerously inshore towards Fort Charles.

"How much room does he need to get out into the open sea?" asked Durkin as the ship came abreast of the schooner on his port side.

Fortunately, Durkin was by far the better seaman and had to steer his ship perilously close between the schooner and the shallows to avert a collision or running ashore. Against the odds he entered harbour safely.

"Damn close thing Mr Durkin" a voice said. It was Captain Oakley who had seen the stupid manoeuvring of the schooner with some alarm. To the experienced eye it seemed to be asking for trouble as well as a lack of seamanship to field such clouds of sail in confined waters.

There were all kinds of small craft criss crossing the harbour that added to the danger and Durkin was unsure where he should steer for. Then Oakley pointed to a Jolly boat flying the harbour masters pennant. A man on her deck signalled to Sea Breeze to follow him and when his intentions were clear Durkin saw he was being led to an empty berth. Once in possession of the facts he took matters into his own hands and ordered all his sails to be 'clewed up'. His arrival had been expected because the sighting of the Sea Breeze off Morant Point had been signalled along the coast to Port Royal and Kingston Harbour. There were five naval barges waiting to take all the cargo destined for the naval base on the sea side of the Cay.

As soon as he had tied up at the quay a naval lieutenant went aboard and explained that all cargos for the naval base were to be discharged on to the barges. He explained that his ratings would stow it on the barges and as far as Oakley was concerned that suited him down to the ground. While the naval cargo went over the port side into the barges all the other goods, including the Welsh slate, the two phaetons for Mr Thadius Markham of Falmouth at the opposite end of the island and the church bell for St Andrew's in the town was lowered over the starboard side on to the quayside. The ship rose visibly quite quickly in the water as she was lightened and Mr Andretti had to take in the slack on the mooring ropes. Captain Oakley was impressed by the speed the discharging was going but he was still unsettled by the mixed readings he was receiving from the barometer. He thought of the long voyage home and decided to allow the crew ashore for a couple of hours in two lots.

This was an opportunity for the cook, Haydon Bailey, to stock up with his secret magic ingredient, pulped cassava root juice, which he used as a food preservative. He knew that meat boiled in the liquid could be kept for indefinite periods. This was a method discovered by the Caribs and was the basis of their 'pepper pot' dish and, provided the liquid was brought to the boil each day, the meat retained its freshness. As the contents of the pot were eaten new ingredients were added and the whole cycle continued. It was little wonder that a good cook, being the custodian of the ship's larder, was an asset to the captain as well as being a comfort to the crew.

It was a relief to Oakley to be rid of the last cargoes and take on the new consignments for England. The men ashore made for the brothels and drinking dens close to the dock and their escapades would fill hours of monotony in the telling on the homeward run. Tom Berry had 'instructed' Zak on the hazards inherent in visiting brothels so the lad was well aware of the dangers he faced. Most of the dives were not only dens of iniquity as described by the clergy but also places of 'festering diseases' described by the better informed.

The next cargos were being assembled on the quay and were more uniform in character than the outward-bound lot. There were more kegs of tobacco, more vats of rum and molasses all of which would stow neatly in the holds. There were 500 stacks of the rare and coveted Bermuda cedar, a wood prized by architects and interior designers in England. It would neatly fill up the void between the kegs and barrels up to the underside of the hatches. It all looked like a full cargo for England and good profits for the ship owners. The seamen hadn't returned to the ship to allow mates to go ashore and Mr Turley, the third mate, assisted by the boson's mate, were ordered to go and round them up. Zak and Tom Berry were allowed ashore for two hours the following day 'to stretch their legs' which was no time at all to explore this busy and thriving port.

The very nature of the cargo meant that loading would be a speedier operation and Captain Oakley decided all should be loaded for midday on the third day. He was getting more confused by the barometer readings and consulted Mr Durkin on the matter. The latter thought there was stormy weather in the offing and both men decided to take extra precautions when they put to sea.

The hatches were battened down for the long run home and the deck felt solid, compact and buoyant underfoot. Mr Dainty was feeling quite useful now that he had demonstrated that he could organise the discharging of the cargo in an orderly manner. His confidence, self assurance and decisiveness had come to maturity It was noticeable that he had changed and that he had grown up in the last weeks. It was clear to the crew and his superiors that here was a young man who showed good officer material. He had found in his nature a masked humility that enabled him to get things done willingly without sounding bossy or superior.

Oakley decided to exit the Caribbean via the Mona Pass between the east coast of Hispaniola and Puerto Rica and out into the Atlantic. In more certain times he might have taken the shorter route between Cuba and Haiti but with the barometer playing up he wouldn't want to get blown into the spread of the Turks and Caicos Islands. He was still preoccupied with the weather and the barometer readings that seemed more confused than ever. Durkin had been reading up on the hurricanes that built up in that part of the world and came across a little rhyme that was apparently composed to make it easier to remember the way of the hurricanes. It read,

June too soon. July stand by. August it must. September remember. October all over.

If only it was as simple as that thought Durkin. He recognised that the verse must have some basis in fact for someone to even think of writing it down and he mentioned it to the captain.

"Perhaps the weather conditions further west are building up to something of a blow sir" commented Durkin.

"Well, it is the 15 of August Mr Durkin...." He said, referring to the verse,

".... but I doubt if the elements that form the weather have heard of your rhyme let alone read it" he said by way of putting the verse into context.

There was a silence as this remark brought Mr Durkin up against a brick wall. Then the captain added,

"But I do accept this is the season for such hurricanes Mr Durkin and that is why I have decided to head straight out for the Atlantic. I'd rather be caught out in open water than in amongst the islands with the constant danger of being driven on the rocks somewhere. What say you Mr Durkin?"

Durkin felt a lot better now, knowing that the captain hadn't dismissed him out of hand.

The truth was that all the conditions required to bring about a hurricane were already coming together a couple of hundred miles out in the South Atlantic. The water was warm, the moisture in the air was rising and the wind pattern near the surface of the ocean was stirring. The air began spiralling inwards and in a short time this caused bands of thunderstorms that had the effect of warming the air further while causing it to rise higher into the atmosphere.

There was no way the captain could have known that he would be heading into the storm until it was travelling towards him. Yes, there might well be a storm, so what? He had encountered storms many times before in his travels and it was a case of waiting to see what turned up. He had ordered every available square foot of sail, including his royals and upper top gallants, to get out of the Caribbean with all speed and into the open Atlantic.....otherwise, everything was going to plan. There was optimism in the air and a light heartedness among the crew who must have been thinking that within the fortnight they would be safely home with their families and loved ones.

During that night the wind got stronger from the south west and Mr Turley, the officer on watch, thought it best not to take in the royals and top gallants in case it caused the ship to reduce speed. Oakley was fast asleep and didn't notice the sudden steep rise in pressure and the finger pointing to 'stormy' on the barometer. It suddenly began to rain like it never rained before and the wind was coming from east to west with growing force straight at the ship. Questions began to nag at Mr Turley and he was in two minds as to whether he should waken the captain. He decided to wait and see but very soon the ship was in the middle of a storm and being tossed like a cork on the waves. The movement became so violent that the captain, Durkin and Andretti appeared on deck together and looking very alarmed. The rain was coming down so heavily that it became difficult to see beyond the mizzen mast in the dark and waves were crashing down on the deck with increasing ferocity.

"Take in the royals and top gallants Mr Turley" shouted the captain but his words were lost in the roar of the wind.

Men came staggering on deck and the boson and his mate urged them to climb aloft and do what they knew to be necessary. As they tried to make for the rat lines to climb up the mast they were swept across the deck by crashing waves which swept them across the deck to the other side.

"Get aloft you men and reef those sails" screamed the captain as men tried to regain their footing.

Some men managed to get on the rat lines but the wind had increased further to such an extent that the ship was now being blown perilously over on her port side. Oakley was fearing the worst fully believing that the cargo in the hatch had not only come adrift but had shifted, thereby causing her to list dangerously on to her side. Durkin had taken the helm to try to bring her head around into the sea but the force of the wind in the sails prevented the rudder from having any influence in controlling the direction of the vessel.

Mr Daynty and Tom Berry had managed to reach the quarter deck and were holding fast to anything that looked a permanent structure. Suddenly, the night lit up as lightning cut through the darkness followed by a deafening thunder. In the instant flash of light men could be seen in the rigging holding grimly on to dangling ropes but unable to move due to the crazy angle of the ship. Another lightning flash showed other men which way they should proceed and further giant waves rolled over the deck. The ship was swept upright just as another flash of lightning lit up the night. The sails looked ghostly and terror could be seen in the eyes of the men trying to take in the sails. In the same moment the worst happened when the top of the main mast was broken like a weathered twig. It was now hanging by the various ropes and was having an adverse effect on the ships stability. There were still men hanging on while others had been blown or washed into the sea. Two luckier ones had fallen on to the deck but were being swilled from one side to the other by the waves washing over the deck. They appeared lifeless, as they made no attempt to help themselves.

Although by now the storm was blowing at over 100 miles an hour Mr Daynty was feeling guilty as he hung on to the helm with Mr Durkin. He knew that he should be doing something to help but what? Suddenly he struggled down to the well deck and made his way to the lifeless figures that had been swept to the port gunwale. He managed to get the end of a flapping rope and tie them to a structure to save them from being washed overboard. He took a axe and knife from one of them and although the ship was practically lying on her side he got a footing on the inboard side of the ratlines. Durkin and the captain shouted to him not to be try to climb the mast but their voices were lost in the storm.

By this time the masts were almost horizontal as they leant over the sea but Mr Daynty went ahead. He reached the top gallant cross tree and although trying to hang on for dear life he began to cut away the ropes that were holding the broken mast. A flash of lightning revealed that two men were trapped under the hanging mast where it had snapped. He could see their plight and saw that they were helpless to lift the weight off themselves. The lad persevered and made his tortuous way up to the break and brought the axe into play. He chopped through the mast while trying to maintain his precarious hold but it seemed like an impossible task. Several times he nearly lost his footing and the frequent flashes of lightning merely emphasised the dire straights the ship was in.

He chopped wildly at the break and suddenly it parted but it was now hanging by rigging ropes. He tackled the ropes with the knife then suddenly it came adrift and was taken away by the following wave. The ship righted herself by only two or three degrees but it was enough for the helm to have some effect in controlling the direction of the ship. The trapped men seemed paralysed with terror and were rooted to the spot. There was another flash of lightning and Zak caught sight of Tom Berry only a few feet below him and clinging to the lower mast. Zak pointed above him to the two men and gestured to Tom that they should bring them down to the deck. Without hesitation, the two lads reached the men and had to wrench the seamen from their grip of terror. They seemed to get a new zest for life and with the help of the midshipman and the cadet they managed to reach the deck with a modicum of safety. The wind had increased further to something like 120 miles per hour and the waves were such that they could swamp the ship and sink her at any time. She was being blown back eastward and Durkin remembered the captain's words when he said he didn't want to get blown ashore on the Turks and Caicos Islands. Hopefully, he thought, they were a long way off them yet.

Durkin caught sight of the captain's eyes and there was nothing but suppressed despair. As for himself, he had never experienced anything like this in all his years at sea. Tom and Zak were joined by Mr Hurley and between them they were able to get the two men out of the weather and into the officer's quarters. By this time it was clear that it was a waste of time trying to reef the sails as most of them had been torn to ribbons but

Durkin still found it impossible to bring the ship's head around into the sea. Fortunately, the ship had righted herself having cheated the wind of acres of sail. Dawn broke and the little daylight that managed to filter through the storm clouds was a great relief. It was clear that most of the sails had been shredded and the rigging that was still in place was blowing freely in the wind. The broken mast would have to be replaced and the spare sails brought out just to reach Liverpool. The waves at this point were gigantic and were washing across the ship more frequently. There was little else the men could do in the circumstances but they were still on standby in case anything else cropped up.

Meantime Mr Turley had gone to see what he could do for the two men who had fallen to the deck but sadly they had expired. He then informed the boson and the sail maker to remove the bodies from the officer's quarters as soon as they could and prepare them for a sea burial when the storm abated. The ship was still in great danger but the hatch covers were holding up well. The storm had also found a weak spot in the captain's quarters where the force of the sea had penetrated one of his state room windows and flooded the place out. The carpenter was on the job almost immediately and was able to shore up the window. A quick count indicated that five men had been swept overboard from the breaking mast but there had been nothing that could have been be done to save them. To make matters worse, the captain had no idea of his present position and would have to wait until he could see the sun or the stars in a clear sky before he could take his bearings.

Tom Berry was on his way to report to the captain that the two men being prepared for burial were Sam Meadows, a father of seven children and Joe Peeler. Both men were from Liverpool. It was then that Tom saw the soaked, lifeless and bedraggled body of Satan, the oldest of the ship's cats, lying in the gully by the gunwales. As the day drew on the hurricane lost none of its ferocity but when the ship was blown over she always managed to regain an even keel. The crew reported that water was leaking into the fo'castle and Oakley suspected that the force of the waves had washed out all the oakum between the bow planking. Mr Durkin looked exhausted as he struggled with the helm but the wind was still too strong on the beam to bring her around into the sea.

Zak suddenly came to realise what he had done and how stupid he had been in climbing the mast in such weather. He knew it took all his nerve to climb the ratlines when the ship was tied up alongside the quayside but to climb up in the face of a hurricane was sheer suicide. Although he was the son of a vicar, it didn't necessarily follow that he was a zealot regarding his religion but he had never seen weather like this before. He realised that men were virtually helpless in these conditions and that it was only natural for them to turn their thoughts and pleas for deliverance to a higher being. They were at the mercy of the elements and deep down in his soul Zak had accepted that the ship could founder at any time and all would be lost to the deep. Something spiritual had urged him, against all odds, to try to cut the top mast away and save the two trapped seaman but he didn't know what. He tried to recall the details of the time when Jesus was in the boat with his frightened disciples at the height of the tempest and the trust they had in him. He now wished he had read more of the bible and taken more notice of his father in church but ...... young minds would rather dream of colour and sunshine and other things.

On the third day the storm blew over and the captain was able to get a fix on his position. The crew were so relieved to have survived the terror that they settled down to repairing the mast, the rigging and the sails. Captain Oakley decided to leave the top mast until he reached Liverpool and to concentrate on getting as much sail as was possible.

When Tom and Zak retired to their hammocks Tom joked about their ordeal but Zak knew he really didn't mean it.

"Tell me Tom, why did you climb the mast in the storm?" Zak asked quietly.

Tom paused to think of an answer but he couldn't find one to replace the truth.

"Well Zak, to be honest, when I saw you scrambling along the ratlines I thought you were going to perish for certain knowing how you feared climbing the masts so I followed you, against my better judgement, in case you needed a hand....and that is the truth" said Tom solemnly casting his eyes down as if not wanting to continue.

Nothing further was said as the two lads gave some thought to the shipmates who had been swept overboard and remembered all of them in their prayers before falling asleep in their hammocks. The captain had decreed that Sam Meadows and Joe Peeler would have a Christian committal and Mr Andretti was put in charge of the arrangements, notwithstanding that time was of the essence. The helm was now back in control and the bow of Sea Breeze was turned into the sea and a course, north, north- east was set for England.......

CHAPTER 8

Homeward Bound

The weather on the following day had moderated and the ship was now well clear of the hurricane. She was fielding an array of odd make-do and-mend sails and as she left the Bahamas far behind on her after port beam she was fortunate enough to catch the wind blowing up from the south Atlantic. It was the day of the funeral and the ship's carpenter had built a dais on the port side in readiness to receive the bodies of Sam Meadows and Joe Peeler later in the day. There was a sombre air among the crew who had obviously made a special effort to dress in a manner befitting the respect they held for the departed. Captain Oakley was a God fearing man on the quiet but never wore his religion on his sleeve. He would have preferred not to have had a funeral service but in the circumstances it was the only way forward. After giving the matter some thought he called Mr Andretti and Mr Daynty to his quarters to assist in drawing up the 'order of burial' service. Two hours before the sun went down the bodies were brought up on deck and placed on the dais.

The crew was called to assembly at the ship's side and presently the captain arrived. The outline of the bodies was clear under the canvas and one could make out the ingots of pig iron taken from the bilge ballast to ensure the bodies quickly sank to the deep. Tom had seen the boson who had agreed to place the pathetically small bundle of the body of Satan between Joe Peeler's feet. The captain looked about him and thought, there, but for the grace of God, how many more lives might have been lost in the storm. He began to speak in a husky voice as he was anxious to put this episode into the past as quickly as possible.

"We have come through a terrifying ordeal and for that we must thank god for our own deliverance. However, the Almighty has saw fit, in his infinite wisdom, and for reasons known only unto himself, that the time was nigh for our shipmates to join him in another place" after a pause he continued,

"We are here gentlemen, to bid farewell to our lost shipmates,
Billy Coote, Alfie Barns, Ted Hayer, Denis Falconer and Manny Henson all of whom were swept overboard at the height of the storm and Sam Meadows and Joe Peeler who fell from the yard arm to the deck and here lie before us…."

He paused again for a brief moment and added,

"… I have been asked to mention our faithful old friend, Satan, the ship's cat, who has been with us since he was a straggling kitten and brought aboard by one of the seamen in Egypt some eleven years ago. He has been faithful through those years and served the ship well and has gone through many storms with us. Alas, old age caught up with him and he was no longer able to navigate through the recent hurricane. I'm sure we will all miss him" he said as he turned the page in the prayer book to read from his notes,

"And now, Mr Zakaria Daynty, our cadet, who is the son of the Rev Joshua Daynty of St Mark's parish in Cheshire, has agreed to read Psalm 130, otherwise known as the De profundis"

Zak took the holy book, somewhat nervously, from the captain and all eyes turned to face him. Suddenly he was overcome with nervous doubt and he felt the blood of youth rushing to his cheeks. There was a pause which seemed to last for ever as he tried to compose himself. He suddenly had a vision of his father

who was just about to give a sermon from the pulpit. From that moment on, he drew strength and purpose and his voice was firm and resolute as he began to read.

"Out of the depths have I cried unto thee, O Lord; Lord hear my voice. And let thine ears be attentive to the voice of my supplication.

If thou, O Lord, shalt observe iniquities; Lord, who shall endure it?

For with thee there is merciful forgiveness: and by reason of thy law I have waited for thee, O Lord.

My soul hath relied on his word; my soul hath hoped in the Lord.

From the morning watch even until night, let Israel hope in the Lord.

Because with the Lord, there is mercy, and with him plentiful redemption.

And he shall redeem Israel from all his iniquities.

Eternal rest give unto them, O Lord. And let perpetual light shine upon them and may they rest in peace"

The quiet confident voice of the cadet seemed to have touched the inner spiritual depths of all those present and they all answered solemnly,

"Amen"

Although Zack's words and phrases were above the rough-hewn and uncultured minds of the seamen, he had impressed them greatly. There were some gleaming tears in the eyes of the men as they gazed on the lifeless forms of their friends sewn into their canvas shrouds. Even Paddy Ireland, who had made a special effort to look respectable, had cleaned his false teeth in some of the cassava preserving liquid from the galley. He tried very hard to look normal and composed, but his teeth were so ill fitting it looked as if his mouth was full of pebbles. His friend, Abel Mannet, who often shared the teeth with him, stood behind him, his toothless face looking gaunt and hollow. The breeze blew stiffly across the deck and the men were brought face to face with their own mortality.

Mr Andretti placed the violin under his chin.

"And now, we will sing the hymn….'Eternal Father strong to save…' accompanied by Mr Andretti on his violin" said the captain.

They sang lustily and with feeling but the line containing the words… 'O hear us er we cry to thee, for those in peril on the sea' had a certain poignancy about them which cut deep into the hearts and minds of every man as the memory of the hurricane dominated their thoughts.

It was now the time for the captain's unsavoury task to make the last stitch to let it be seen that the men were in fact dead. He took hold of the needle in his right hand then felt for the nose of Sam Meadows and pushed the needle through the soft tissue in his nostrils below the nasal bone. There was no reaction from the deceased so he tied a knot and the boson cut it with a knife. The captain repeated the last stitch on Joe Peeler and as expected, there was no response.

"And it is now my sad duty to commit our friends to the deep. Into thy hands O Lord, we commend their spirits and may they rest in peace" he concluded reverently as the dais was tipped and the bodies slipped into the sea.

Captain Oakley was relieved that the funeral was over and wanted to concentrate on getting home. The men dispersed quietly and returned to their duties. Tom and Zack retired to their cabin and Tom congratulated Zack on his reading of the psalm.

"You were just like a real vicar Zack" he commented but Zack could only smile wanly.

It became all too clear that the ship was making slow headway under inadequate sails when another vessel coming up from the south Atlantic seemed to fly past on Sea Breeze's starboard side. She was the 1.498 [old tons] clipper 'Witch of the Wave' en route from Canton to Dungeness with a valuable cargo of tea and crates of china ware. She was lucky to have trailed the recent hurricane and would, no doubt, reach England days ahead of Sea Breeze.

The captain went to great lengths to record as much of the damage to the ship, as a result of the hurricane, the loss of members of his crew and of course the funeral. No doubt, the owners would let it be known how much it had all cost them and they would make sure that the crew also knew how generous they were holding the service and supplying the were-with-all to bury the dead. He also made some pertinent and highly praiseworthy notes regarding Mr Daynty.

"It has become very clear to my self and my officers that in Mr Daynty, there is the making of a good seaman and a fine officer.

He displayed a rare courage for such a young man when he climbed the mast, which was already lying horizontally out over the ocean, and cut the broken top mast free. His action brought the ship back to a more even keel but it had posed a real dander to his life.

He does have a way with the men who are only too willing to carry out tasks at his behest and I can envisage him becoming master of his own vessel at an early age. I have consulted with Mr Durkin who suggests that the midshipman, Tom Berry, should be promoted to third mate next voyage in place of Mr Turley and that Mr Daynty should become midshipman, at least for another voyage. I shall write out a reference to Mr Elias Tallon, our shareholder, who asked me for such a report on the lad and how he has taken to the sea. In short, I can see that Mr Daynty has a promising career as an officer in the royal naval service and his enlisting will be Sea Breezes loss"

For the next seven days the ship made slow progress and sighted at least six ships on their outward bound voyages and they must have guessed that Sea Breeze had been through some very rough weather. They passed the Ambrose lighthouse off the Scillies and captain Oakley ordered everything to be done that would enhance the ship's appearance for entering Liverpool. Sixteen hours later Sea Breeze was sighted off the South Stack then presently, the North Stack lighthouse came into view. The sea was choppy right into Liverpool bay but things calmed down as the ship entered the River Mersey.

There was great relief as she tied up at the Alfred Quay and the gangway was pushed out ashore. The men were paid off and told to report back in a week's time. One of them, Eddy Cane, was laden down with his gear and newly acquired artefacts with the deceased Sam Meadow's St Vincent parrot perched on his shoulders. He had taken it upon himself to deliver it to Sam's son who lived two streets away from him.

Zak was glad to see his two elder sisters Penny and Rachel and his father who had come to meet him. He took them to his cabin and introduced them to Tom but it was too crowded to hold all of them.

"Did you get my letter I sent from Trinidad father" Zak asked

"No, I didn't son"

"That's odd because I sent it on the Greyhound which was homeward bound when we were in Port of Spain" he said sounding very disappointed.

"Ah! The Greyhound, now it all becomes clear to me Zak. I'm afraid The Greyhound foundered in a hurricane and was sunk with the loss of all hands. The wreckage was washed ashore across Anguilla, St Martin and Barbuda in the Leeward Islands and was identified by her figurehead of a greyhound but nothing more was heard of her again"

Zak shook his head in disbelief and said,

"Well, I never thought she would have been caught up in the same storm but she must have encountered it early in its development.

We must have sailed into it later on but it was a terrible storm father because we lost most of our sails as well as seven members of our crew"

They spoke at length then it was time to go ashore. When they went up on deck they met the captain.

"You have a fine son in Mr Daynty sir" said the captain to the clergyman.

"Thank you captain" replied Zak's father as the family made their was ashore to the waiting carriage.

"And as for you Mr Daynty, I hope to see you back here in three weeks time... as the midshipman"

This was a surprise to Zak who thanked the captain then joined his waiting family in the coach.

As the coach travelled through the Cheshire lanes, Zak was quiet as he thought how beautiful the countryside was in late autumn. He realised how much he had missed the scenery and how he had always taken it for granted. He was having trouble with his thoughts and some decisions that would have to be resolved as soon as possible.

"A penny for them Zak" his father asked.

Zak was in deep thought and was taken by surprise.

"Errrrr, Oh, I was just thinking how lovely the countryside looks"

"Yeeeees, it is pretty isn't it" replied his father knowing full well that something was troubling him…..

And his father was right. Zak had seen and heard many things he would never have encountered had he not travelled to the Caribbean and it had given him much food for thought. He had come face to face with the power of the Almighty, as well as his mercy, but the mysteries surrounding the human understanding of the ways of God were challenging and no less mystifying. He had become drawn, but not yet overtly, to all things spiritual and he began to question his future career at sea. He still wanted to serve in the navy and knew he could make a valuable contribution to the nation as a naval officer, a dream that had been with him since he could remember, but he had reached a fork in the path of his young life. He would be seventeen on 3rd of October and there wasn't a lot of time to decide which way he should proceed. He was mindful of the help and encouragement he had received from such people as Captain Oakley, Mr Elias Tallon, one of the shareholders in The Sea Breeze, Mr Fallowfield, Mr Durkin, Tom Berry and of course his father. They had all placed their faith in him and here he was thinking of giving it all up but what would his decision be? ……

And now, they were driving through the familiar lanes of Tarmley Edge and the sounds of the horse's hooves, making contact with the cobble stones underfoot, broke the silence of the countryside with their regular rhythm. Presently the rhythm was broken as the carriage drew up outside the Manse. His mother was waiting to greet him and she hugged him closely and led him into the house. Zak breathed in deeply of the safe atmosphere of his childhood and he was glad to be home. He noted the same antimacassars draped over the backs of the chairs that lent a sense of permanence and safety to the manse. They waited in the reception room while Mrs Laurie, the housekeeper, finished making the dining room ready. The Rev. Daynty accepted a sherry from his wife and he suddenly thought that perhaps Zak might appreciate a glass.

"Would you care to join me Zak" asked his father but Zak declined.

They were eagerly waiting to hear of his exploits in foreign parts but Zak just wanted to soak up the atmosphere of his home. Presently, Betty Amlett, the dining room maid entered and informed Mrs Daynty that everything was now ready.

"Dinner is about to be served Father. Shall we go in?" she invited.

As they entered the dining room, Zak saw that several relations and family friends were already seated and they clapped heartily as he took his place next to his father who sat at the head of the table.

Dinner went without a hitch and there was lots of talking and discussion on all manner of topics but Zak was quiet as he wrestled with his thoughts. Someone even likened Zak's young life to Admiral Lord Nelson as being the son of a clergy man and a career in the navy. It was even hinted at that Zak might well end up an admiral. His father got to his feet and welcomed Zak home, thanking god he was returned to the family safe and sound. To emphasise the point he mentioned the letter he didn't receive.

"Zak wrote me a letter from Port of Spain when his ship first made landfall outward bound but, my friends, I never received that letter. You see, the ship that was bringing it to England was caught up in a hurricane some time later and foundered in the Atlantic with the loss of all hands. I tell you this, my friends, because much later on in the voyage, that same storm caught up with Zak's ship and seven men were lost. The ship was nearly sunk but thankfully, she managed to weather the storm and return my son to the bosom of his family"

There were murmurings and sighs of satisfaction at his homecoming.

There was an instant reaction to this news when everyone applauded Sak's presence. He knew that he would be asked to say something and he wondered how much of his thoughts he should reveal. Then his father called him to his feet.

"Thank you for this reception my friends and may I reiterate how pleased I am to be here. Most of you will know that during my years growing up I was always intent on following a career in the navy. Indeed, one or two of you, including you Aunt Maude and Aunt Tillie, used to address me as Captain Zak when I was a boy. This only reinforced my hope to make good in the navy and strive for excellence"

Everybody nodded their approval then Zak carried on.

"Captain Oakley and his officers have been a great inspiration to me and they have taught me a lot. The captain has asked me to return to the ship in three weeks time as midshipman on her next voyage"

He stopped speaking as if he was having difficulty deciding on his next sentence. His outlook on life and on his future had gone through a 'renaissance' at the height of the hurricane while he was still struggling up the mast amid the rigging. He hadn't suddenly become disenchanted with a life at sea because it might get dangerous or he might lose his life. Oh no, it had something to do with the fact that he had come face to face with the power of the almighty in that he realised all hands could have perish but for his infinite mercy. He had decided at the time that if he was spared he would dedicate his life to humanity…. He went on,
"The fact is that I now wish to attend theological college then follow my father into the church and become a servant of the people" he said in a matter of fact way and with some relief that he had got it off his chest.

There was dismay on the faces of those present as they turned questioningly to one another. His father was speechless as he could never have imagined his son taking this course of action. There were many of those present who secretly believed that Zak had found the life at sea far too strenuous and uncomfortable and had chosen what he thought to be an the easier option, the clergy….

When all the guests had gone his father sat with him and probed this 'calling to God'. He knew that the captain must be very satisfied with Zak's aptitude and application otherwise he wouldn't have asked him back if he had any doubts. Zak was very forthcoming with his father who had pulled all kinds of strings to get him taken on the Sea Breeze but he now realised that his son was very serious indeed. He would have to get word to Captain Oakley as soon as possible regarding the new situation and to explain his son's thinking……….

The Sea Breeze sailed without him and steps were taken to get Zak a place at theological college. During his time there one of the teachers happened to mention, in passing, that congregations, in general, preferred their ministers to be married men. Ostensibly, this was mainly for practical purposes like the smooth running of the manse but at a deeper level, because they were not 'foot loose and fancy free'. Zak bore this advice in mind and before long he had renewed his friendship with Eloise

Rakes his childhood playmate. They married when he was twenty one and the following year Eloise gave birth to a daughter Margaret. Whilst still at college he received a call from the Manse informing him that his father had suffered a severe heart attack but by the time he reached the manse his father had passed away. There was great sadness in the family and the wider parish and after the funeral the bishop appointed Zak as 'interim incumbent'

After six months Zak was installed as the vicar and his wife took over the responsibility of the manse. She dealt with all aspects of the day to day running of the manse which included the cleaning and administration of the church, instructing the staff, all the correspondence and answering of queries which came to the door. She had set out to protect him from the rigours of running the parish and endeavoured to take on as much of the responsibilities off his shoulders as was possible. They were both surprised how much of a job it was to be the vicar and how little time was left for themselves. But, he had gone into the clergy with his eyes wide open and was always mindful of his promise to serve the people.

One morning, when opening the mail, Eloise came across an odd letter addressed to Mr Zak Daynty. The envelope bore a stamp
post-marked St Lucia and dated 15 May 1861. She held it lightly between her thumb and forefinger and wondered who could be writing from so far away. Perhaps it was from one of the many churches her husband had talked about. She opened it and withdrew six pages. She began to read..

Mrs Anna de Witt Pardo
The Tammeron Plantation
St Lucia
Windward Islands
The British West Indies
!3 May 1861

Dear Zak,
I have wanted to write this letter to you for quite a long time but kept putting it off. I do want to thank you for making my voyage out from England in 1853 a bearable but memorable experience. I can still see you in my mind's eye waving goodbye from the deck of The Sea Breeze as our boat sailed out of the harbour. I am

now married to Fergus James Pardo who manages the plantation and we live on my father's plantation.

I should have told you much earlier that I gave birth to your son, also named Zak, in June 1854. He looks just like you and keeps asking all sorts of questions about you. The plantation is situated eight miles inland so I don't know how he will take to the sea...... like his father"......

Eloise's jaw had dropped and she had to check the envelope to make sure it really was addressed to her husband. She dismissed it as some kind of a mistake at first as she knew her husband was not that sort of man. Even if he had erred, he would have told her as they had both vowed at their wedding that whatever happened in their married life they would always remain faithful and be truthful with each other. She began to wonder if she should carry on reading the letter as it was, to say the least, a little more than personal. She wondered how many times they had made love and why he hadn't told her about it. She read on....

"I have two more children by my husband, Laura five and Benjamin three. The three of them get on well together but Laura and Ben look so different from Zak. I think you should meet him when I go to England in two years time when young Zak will be nine years old. I am enrolling him at The Miss Everts residential school outside Cheltenham. I think it only right and proper that you and your son should know each other at least, and I'm sure you would agree with that"

The rage began to rise in Eloise and the blood rushed to her head. She was angry at the very thought that her chastened marriage had been sullied all the time. She had read enough and exclaimed aloud,
"The cheeky hussy.... now she wants to come and visit him. My God! What will people think?" she ranted as she bundled the crumpled letter and envelope into a desk drawer. She had visions of her life being ruined beyond repair if this...this hussy were allowed to darken the doors of the manse. That must not happen she vowed. Something prompted her to take the letter out again and see how 'Mrs De Witt Pardo' signed herself off. She turned to the last page and read,
"I have missed you dear Zak and often think about you.

I remain
Your loving Anna
X X X "

"Your loving Anna indeed" she echoed haughtily as she crumpled the letter again and shoved it back into the drawer.

"And three kisses to boot. I'll see what he has to say when he finishes the morning service" she said with venom brewing in her heart and not realising she was talking aloud.

She decided to take a walk to calm down and regain her composure before confronting him on the subject....

Zak entered the study and breathed a sigh of relief that the funeral was over. He immediately noticed the absence of Eloise who was usually working at the desk. He noticed the crumpled letter on the desk and took hold of it. He smoothed it out to read the envelope and was somewhat puzzled why his wife might have crumpled it and left it on the desk. He took a closer look at the stamp. It depicted the head of Queen Victoria with the words 'St Lucia Postage' and he proceeded to read the letter. As soon as he saw the name De Witt he guessed who it was from. He read it once and thought about it then read it again. In truth, he had all but forgotten about his liaison with Anna but to be suddenly confronted with a letter from her brought back warm glowing memories of his deep affection he had for her. And now, she informed him, she had borne him a son who would be coming to England to start his proper education.

Suddenly, he realised why his wife wasn't at her desk and the crumpled letter spoke volumes. She was obviously very angry and would, no doubt, bring the issue up as soon as she saw him. It was only then that he understood the relevance of the Roman maxim from his time at theological college, veritas odium parit,....

'Truth breeds hatred'. His thoughts ran on and he wondered what the Romans might have to say about his present dilemma. He recalled that as far as they were concerned, it was not always wise to be frank with one's friends. Perhaps they would have described his present position as being between the devil and the deep blue sea or, a precipice in front, and a pack of rabid wolves behind. What does one do when caught between equally hazardous or difficult alternatives? he asked himself.

Eloise entered the room and sat expressionless at her desk. There was no greeting and she said nothing. Zak waited for her to speak and after a pause she said stonily.

"I see you have got that letter then, from that.... that hussy"

"Errrr yes, I have, but I wouldn't describe Anna as a hussy and it is rather unfortunate since I didn't know about the boy. I was going to tell you about Anna when we got married but then decided to 'let sleeping dogs lie' since it was already in the past and wouldn't have helped"

She said nothing but the expression on her face changed to one of hostility. She thought he'd got it right when he referred to 'sleeping dogs' but she held her council. He wasn't too sure what he should do next but after further silence he read the letter again. Eloise sat and watched the expression change on his face and she seemed to derive a secret satisfaction from his discomfort. She sat po-faced waiting for his explanation.

"Well Eloise, I am sorry for not telling you before but it happened and it is a fact. In the circumstance, I would ask for your forgiveness and since we cannot alter the past to accept it and deal with it as it is and not as we might like it to be. He nearly added that 'none of us was perfect' but he feared that would only add to his dilemma. It took time for Eloise to come to terms with this new dimension to her marriage but she saw that there was a positive side to it. She realised that to dwell on the negative would only trouble her mind way into the future and further hinder their marriage.

When all had settled down, Zak reflected on his Latin studies in college and was reminded that, even the Romans accepted long ago that 'Lovers are lunatics' At least they acknowledged the things that lovers did and considered it justification for this maxim. Those of us who still have our wits about us should take this into account when we are smitten like this. After all, Publilius Syrus advises us that even a god finds it hard to make love and be wise at the same time. God, he thought, the Romans had been through it all before and apparently had learnt how to deal with it…..

The two years were long in passing and Zak had received four more letters from Anna. They were more formal now that she knew he was the vicar of St Marks and was a respectably married man with a young daughter. Eloise battled with her rebellious thoughts but over time, she came to accept that Zak was as vulnerable to the wiles of human nature as anyone else… including herself. She had admitted to herself for one or two secret fancies which went much further than Zak's imagination but she daren't mention them to him. In accepting her failures, she even wrote to Anna offering to let her stay at her mother's house when she came to visit Zak in England. It took that long to come to terms with all the problems arising from Anna's impending visit to be resolved and Zak had to concede that the Romans had found the answer yet again when Ovid, in 'metamorphoses' calls our attention to the irreversible results—both good and bad—of the passage of time. tempus edax rerum…. Time is the devourer of all things.

THE END

Appendix

The following notes are as written in the original story. I feel they give a better understanding to the reader, especially if they have little or no knowledge of life on board a ship in those days.

NB Mercator.

Latin translation of the name of the Flemish born German cartographer Gerhard Kremer [1512—94] Mercator's projection. A representation of the surface of the globe in which the meridians are parallel straight lines, the parallel straight lines at right angles to these, their distances such that everywhere degrees of latitude and longitude have the same ratio to each other as on the globe itself.

Author's Notes

I had intended to finish on chapter three but since the ship, 'Sea Breeze' had only made her first port of call of the voyage there seemed to be a lot more adventure to come for Mr Daynty. I must admit I was tempted to mention the battles of Camperdown and St Vincent in 1793 mainly because that was also the year of the birth of my great, great paternal grandfather who [eventually] farmed 26 acres at Penyffordd Farm in Whitford, Holywell, Flint He died there of paralyses in 1872 at the age of 79.

AUTHOR'S NOTES: On Tuesday, I had written 2500 words and was in the process of thinking through the text to see if there was any part that needed improvement or even inserting additions etc. I thought it would be a good idea to take a 'total' word count. I had just finished counting chapter IV and moving to chapter V but it wasn't there any more. I had saved it repeatedly but I couldn't fine it anywhere. I got a 'knowledgeable' chap in but he agreed with me that I had completely lost it. I have to tell you I was as sick as a dog and dwelt on all that work disappearing. I decided then that I would re-write it as far as I could remember and on

Wednesday morning I got up as usual at 5.30am to start working. I put the radio on and to my dismay I learnt that it wasn't 5.30am but 4.30am. I couldn't remember the text verbatim and had to invent new angles one of which was the love scene in Anna's cabin. However, when it came to the word count I discovered I had written a great deal more than the original.

NOTES

Against all the ship's unwritten rules, a small tight group of older seamen, who had an addictive liking for cheap and roughly brewed rum and other unidentified spirits, had taken the opportunity to secretly stock up with the stuff back in Trinidad. The stuff had been stowed away in the lamp locker [and other hiding places] and was safe enough among the containers of lamp oil. The men felt the need for the drink in the colder northern climate on the homeward bound run when they would take a nightly ration to help them fight the cold as well as to satisfy their addictive needs.

On reaching Liverpool Captain Oakley learns that the schooner Greyhound was presumed to have foundered in a hurricane five days after leaving Port of Spain.

The Rev Daynty is informed that the Sea Breeze will be docking at Liverpool according to the telegraph from Point Lines in Anglesey to Formby then relayed to New Brighton on the Cheshire side of the River Mersey ????

The weather was set fare.......etc..

1854 Lightning. Melbourn to Liverpool 63 days. Wool
Witch of the wave built 1851. 1852 China to England Canton to Dungeness 90 days nb 86 days. Tea. Out of [the river Min] Foochow 1498 'old' tons, length …. She signalling her name , using Marriat's code flags on the mizzen mast

Deep hulled Marco Polo acquired it early in 1852 James Bains of Liverpool who fitted her out for the Australian trade. She had b een built at St John,New Brunswick, Canada in 1851 by James Smith and measured

184.1 feet x 36.3ft x 29.4 ft at 1400 tons old measurement. She had logged [in the past] 22 knots.

ST VINCENT. [21 miles SW of St Lucia and 100 miles West of Barbados St Mary's Roman Catholic [Romanesque with heavy gothic overtones and a very ornate interior.] Cathredral

Next door is the cathredral school. The first church on the site was built between 1823-28 and was extended 1877when the steeple and sanctuary were added and enlarged again in 1891.

NOTES

Zack now has to knuckle down to learn how to read ships charts and will come across such terms as Mercater, Peters and Azymuthal projections as well as learning the seaman's common nomenclature regarding names of all items of equipment.

He will have to climb the masts [via the ratlines etc] to see how the rigging works so that he understands it. He will learn not to order someone to do something he hasn't done or couldn't do himself.

Nb AB Billy Benbow.

HOMEWARD BOUND Chapter VI

One of the sailors [toothless] i.e. Paddy Ireland, [who shares a set of crude false teeth [carved from a piece of whale bone] with a shipmate 'when the meat comes tough' is an alcoholic [the crew think he only drinks more than he should and think no more about it] stocks up with cheap Jamaica rum ......to keep himself warm in the colder climes when homeward bound. He goes aloft one night [when the ship encounters a hurricane] to reef the top sails, misses his footing on the foot rope and falls to the deck.

Author's notes.

I fully intended to write an epic poem of the sea and made many notes of rhyming nautical words in the Wynstay Arms on Monday 21 May 2007. I thought about it knowing full well I am hopeless at writing poetry but where could I start? I put all the words in the computer on Tuesday morning [starting at 5am] but ….. Later in the morning I started to write. I realised I wasn't writing the poem but the story began to flow. I decided to carry on with the story and forgot about the poem. .

NB Satan is the oldest cat on board and is jet black. His territory is the crew's quarters in the fo'castle. Tiger is ginger and his territory is the galley while Moonbeam the youngest lives in the officer's quarters.

Petty officers Bosun Sailmaker [sails] carpenter [chips]

Barquentine A barquentine is a vessel having three or four masts, fully square rigged on the foremast and fore and aft rigged on the remainder. Six- mast

Length 137 , 31 breath , 19ft draught   square rigged. Three masts clipper

Sails Reduce canvas. Yards five. 4 jibs. 'clewed up and drying'

Square rig. A vessel is said to be square-rigged when she has one or more masts with a complete range o square sails. A topsail schooner is not classified as square-rigged as she has only upper square sails.

Printed in Great Britain
by Amazon

39562988R00056